IN CASE
YOU FORGOT

By Frederick Smith

Down For Whatever

Right Side of the Wrong Bed

Play It Forward

Visit us at www.boldstrokesbooks.com

IN CASE
YOU FORGOT

by

Frederick Smith and Chaz Lamar

2019

IN CASE YOU FORGOT

ISBN 13: 978-1-63555-493-9

This Trade Paperback Original Is Published By
Bold Strokes Books, Inc.
P.O. Box 249
Valley Falls, NY 12185

First Edition: June 2019

CREDITS
EDITOR: STACIA SEAMAN
PRODUCTION DESIGN: STACIA SEAMAN
COVER DESIGN BY TAMMY SEIDICK

To those who've taught us a little more about love and loss.
No more reindeer games.

ZAIRE

ICYF: Be Honest

The smell of boiled chicken with Caribbean seasonings lingers around the room as I pour out unspoken feelings across our dining table.

I never liked this dining table, but it made him very happy. The day we chose it, the weekend we moved in with each other, it rained. A random day of rain in the middle of July. I bought way too much for our quaint condo with no air-conditioning. I remember not wanting much myself, all I really wanted was the counter-height dining table. He wanted the old-fashioned mahogany-colored wooden family-style dinner table. He also wanted these wackadoo wooden chairs to accompany. I thought stools would be nice. We inevitably got what brought a smile to his face.

We sit in the kitchen, as the chicken simmers. It hasn't been a full year of living together and here we are.

"So…something is off with me," I say. I've thought about what I could say to soften the truth. But that has been my struggle. Always needing to soften the truth or something for someone else. "With this. With us. I can't quite explain it. But I know, I'm not happy. I think we need to separate. Maybe *not* divorce. But perhaps live apart." That was the softening. Unnecessary in retrospect. I am calm in my speech. I am also sad. I know I cannot take back these words.

Time stands still. We stare at each other in the eyes. I cannot quite read Mario. I know he is processing. I dare not do what I've been accustomed to doing our entire five-year relationship—coddle, challenge, and support. I sit in silence with him.

"When you texted me this afternoon, Zaire, that we should talk tonight," he says, "I thought it was going to be about my birthday. I didn't think you wanted a divorce."

Mario gets up from the table, walks over to the stove, and turns off the fire. Grabs his keys, leaves the kitchen, returns to the kitchen, and looks at me.

"This is how we are ending? Like this?" he asks, more of a statement than a question.

"I didn't say I wanted a divorce."

I do.

"Fuck you, Zaire," he says. "I'm going for a drive. I don't know when I'll be back. Do not check in on me."

The door slams.

I, Zaire James, am the eldest of four. I do everything first. The good, the bad, the unexpected. I figured that's the role the eldest is supposed to have. So whenever I do something I'm sure my other siblings haven't, I cope by telling myself it's supposed to happen this way. I am very close to my siblings. We weren't always so intimate, but when our mother passed away my junior year of college, shit got real, real quick. I was twenty, my sister Savannah was nineteen, the middle girl Langston was seventeen, and the baby boy Harlem was fifteen. Our father was murdered by an undercover cop during our childhood. I was there. I was also nine and this was before body cameras, live cell phone recordings, and #BlackLivesMatter. There weren't any riots or major news coverage. There was, however, our neighborhood and community love. I remember for a month, our home was filled with flowers and food from our block and local community. Then there was a settlement and we moved from South Central, now known as South L.A. or SoLa, #gentrification, to this white town in the high desert, hoping to start a new life, where no one knew our names, our past, our trauma.

I sit at the table alone for a few minutes, not knowing exactly what to do next. I am sad and at the same time, I feel a breath of relief that I had spoken a truth that was buried deep for a few months.

Fuck you.
I thought it was going to be about my birthday. I didn't think
you wanted a divorce.
I didn't think you wanted a divorce.
I didn't think.
That is what he should have said. I. Didn't. Think. How much
of myself did he need? How much more of myself did he want? This
condo, in the San Fernando Valley, his desire. The alkaline water
machine, the Alexa, the bidet, these other gadgets that fill our home,
his desire, his want, his command. Fuck me. The audacity. I know
that *fuck you* was from a place of hurt. I will try not to hold on to that
fuck you. I will try not to get angry.
Fuck you.
Then there are tears on my face. Some on this table where I sit.
Alone.
The smell of the chicken that I do not actually want brings
me back to myself. I text Savannah, Langston, and Harlem in our
sibling group chat: JamesGang.

> *Zaire: Happy Monday. I'm getting a divorce. Another*
> *first. Drinks tomorrow night?*

I know Harlem will be the first to reply. I turn off my phone
before I get a notification. I get up from the table. Turn off the
kitchen light. Leaving the chicken in the pot, I grab my car keys.
I do what I have done for years when I do not know what to do,
but I know I must do. I drive west. I end up at the ocean.
Yes, getting a divorce is shitty, and yet it feels fitting. I wonder
who in my circle will be next. Tragic.

KENNY

ICYF: Leave On Read

I'm in Toledo. He's in Los Angeles. I'm in the back of a limo, just minutes away from the church, where my two sisters and I will give the performance of a lifetime as we say goodbye for the final time to the one who gave us life—our mother. Texts from family members have been coming in all morning, but it's the one from him—Brandon-Malik—that I've looked forward to the most. It's been well over a week. I tap and open his text.

Brandon-Malik (heart emoji): This is going to be a novel, four page letter, Kenny, so bear with me. Lol.

I hope you are doing well. You've probably noticed that I've pulled away and distanced myself from you since you went back home for...you know what. Ten days is the most that we've gone without seeing, talking, or being with each other, especially after spending so much time together in the past year.

I want to give you space while you deal with your situation with your mom. Part of it is for me, too. I just don't know how to support someone who's going through what you're going through. I've never had someone significant in my life die and I don't know if

I'm going to do or say the wrong thing. So, I guess, in a way I'm taking the easy way out by just not saying or doing anything. I apologize if this hurts you.

You are amazing. I hope one day we can pick up where we left off, but for now, I think the best thing is for both of us to have space. It's not you, it's me. Don't forget how much I love you, respect you, like you, and like being with you. For now...let me give you space until the time feels right for me and when you're back to...yourself again.
B

Trigger fingers me. I text back right away.

Kenny: Hey B. I am happy and sad to hear from you. Happy that you've reached out, finally. Sad that you say you want space.

No explanation needed.

No one knows how to support someone who's lost their mother. Just reach out now and then, even with this space you want. I'd love and appreciate that from you.

If you don't know what to say, just send an emoji that expresses what you're thinking or feeling. I'll know what you mean. Or that you're just thinking about me. That's better than nothing. I just want to know you're there for me. Especially after all we've done and been to each other.

I miss you. I miss us. I've wondered why the disappearing act. Now I know why. I'll be back in

L.A. in a few weeks, but I'll be ready to pick up where we left off. If you want. I hope you want.

I love you.
K

The limo door opens and I see a receiving line of family and friends all dressed in black and violet, ready to greet my sisters and me at the church. They're here to celebrate my dear mother's life. Little do they know that I just got broken up with via text message. That's no way to say goodbye. Tragic.

SUMMER

KENNY

ICYF: Hear Your Friends

I'm about to stop being nosy from watching the moving truck parked across the street from my place for two reasons. One, because I've got some black beans, quinoa, and spinach that I'm cooking for lunch and I don't want them to burn. Two, because I hear my phone chime to notify that I've got an incoming text message.

The last week of every month—with people coming and going from the neighborhood—is always interesting in West Hollywood. But it's especially interesting once June's Pride Month festivities have ended and people, fresh off a month-long binge of parties, performances, and parades, think living here will replicate that celebratory feeling. Hasn't been my case, and I'm a good three weeks living in WeHo myself.

I'm looking for new people who might become friends, since moving to WeHo—also known as the gayborhood of the city—from the east side suburbs of Los Angeles. Between the mix of Black, Latinx, and Asian Pacific Islander people moving items from the truck I've been watching, I can't tell if I'm finally going to get some more color in this neighborhood or if the people I see are working for yet another white guy, white straight couple, or white blah blah blah moving into WeHo. I'll have to get back to watching this storyline of the new neighbors unfold in a few minutes before my lunch overcooks.

I make my way across the gray laminate hardwood floor from the living room picture window to the kitchen, when I hear another text notification. I'm shook. This time it's the special tone *we* use with each other. A tone I haven't heard in weeks, since shortly after my graduation party and the day of...I don't want to think about that day right now. Brandon-Malik has gone ghost. For weeks. And now he's texting. Again. Ugh. Shit. Damn.

I turn off the burners, and despite being hungry—starving, in fact—I head toward my phone, which I think is still inside my gym bag on the kitchen-adjacent barstool. It's definitely a text from Brandon-Malik, but I don't know if I should leave it unread, read it and not respond, or just see what the first text—a group text from my doctoral classmates—longtime best friend Carlos and our straight girlfriends Tyra and Lily are messaging me about on a Saturday morning.

I open the group text from Carlos, Tyra, and Lily first:

> *Carlos: Kenny. Meet us for brunch at the Abbey at 12:30. We're parched. Ricky is in Palm Springs for the weekend with his softball team.*

I reply.

> *Kenny: I just made lunch...And deciding if I should read this text I just got from Brandon-Malik or not.*
> *Tyra: Fuck BM and find a doctor to fuck.*

By the way, Tyra calls Brandon-Malik "BM" because she says he's a piece of shit.

> *Lily: Open it. Fuck BM. Forget him.*
> *And meet us at the Abbey. Been too long. Wanna see how you been.*
> *Tyra: And why is he texting now anyway? He been ghost since your mom died last month anyway. Fuck him.*
> *Carlos: I'm Lyfting over to your place in WeHo now. So you gotta go. No excuses. Deuces.*
> *Lily: Not like we got homework anymore. We doctors now.*

Tyra: Dr. Kane. Me and Lily on the way. Meet you at the Abbey.

I reply: *You're right. All right. See you in an hour...*

Carlos: See you in ten minutes, Doc. My Lyft is exiting Santa Monica right now.

So much for black beans, quinoa, and spinach today, but hey, that's dinner for later.

What does Brandon-Malik want? Ugh. Let me see. Part of me is excited that he's contacted me. Part of me is wondering why now. I press his name.

BM (shit emoji):

Oh, I've shortened Brandon-Malik's name, like Tyra, to "BM" and added a shit emoji next to his name.

Hi (hello emoji)

Hi? Freaking hi.

And so now, six weeks later, after absolutely no response to my accommodating or excusing what I now see as Brandon-Malik's lame excuse to end things with me, he decides to text *Hi.*

Hi.

The fuck? I'm shook. Six weeks. And this.

Happy that Brandon-Malik texted. Sad that Brandon-Malik texted. I'm leaving the message on "read." That'll send him a message without sending one. I set the phone aside, wondering if I'll get anything else from Brandon-Malik. I kinda hope so. I do miss him. A lot.

I am this close to one of those going-down-memory-lane moments, where, if this were a TV show, I'd see a bunch of flashbacks scroll across the screen—the casual glance across the gym floor, his basketball games at the nearby park, the first time he liked a few pictures and dropped into my social media DMs, texting and FaceTiming to learn more about each other before a series of food, concert, and Netflix and chill dates. Those are the good going-down-memory-lane moments. The bad ones, which I don't like to think about often—being nosy about his social media likes and follows, the photos and videos of him with other cute and younger-than-me men, the times between our dates when he's with other dates, and more—I wouldn't want to include in the TV show flashback scene of our time together. But they're there, I know, and part of the story of me—Kenny Kane—and him—Brandon-Malik.

Meantime, cut to present scene from flashbacks, I Tupperware all the vegan cuisine I just prepped and place it in the fridge, peek out the front window again to catch a glimpse of who my new neighbors might be, and head to the shower. Looking forward to what, if anything, Brandon-Malik might text next, but for now… I've got a brunch date with Carlos, Tyra, and Lily at the Abbey, and hopefully, I'll give a West Hollywood neighborly hello to whoever's moving in across the street after I've had a few libations.

❖

"I should probably be venting to a therapist instead of venting to you all," I tell Carlos, Tyra, and Lily, full of spirit that comes with a third frosé and hardly any food. "My life is a mess."

Carlos, I've known for way over a decade. My bestie at work, when we were entry-level professionals—him in campus activities; me in diversity work at California University, East Los Angeles (CUELA)—and then eventually moving up the student affairs career ladder. And besties outside of work, playing softball, running, barhopping (in our twenties), and man collecting—him with his long-term partner, Ricky, through whom I met my first serious ex, DaVon. That's another story.

Having already been friends, Carlos and I bonded pretty quickly with Tyra and Lily when we started in our doctoral program in educational leadership three and a half years ago. My three favorite classmates, we graduated together just six weeks ago. One day, like magic, we bonded in a class on statistics and research methods by deciding to use their Tinder swipes left and right as the measures for our class project. From there, with our similar interests in social justice and lamenting the state of being woke millennial scholars of color in L.A., Carlos, Tyra, Lily, and I were a tight trio of friends and scholars in a cohort of eighteen classmates. They knew all about Brandon-Malik, as I'd known about the men who were coming in and out of their lives and beds while we were doctoral students.

After telling them about what the previous six weeks had been for me—handling everything that comes with the death of a parent, quitting my job, turning down a lucrative job offer to be an associate vice president at a community college, venturing out into the unknown business of consulting, working for myself and the possibility of having no work at all, packing up and selling my house in Monterey Park and moving to a small condo in WeHo, wondering what to make of Brandon-Malik's ghosting and reappearance text— this brunch and beverage session was what I thought I needed. Or was it?

"That's what I get falling for an IG model," I say and signal to our server that I'm ready for a fourth frosé that I'll probably regret later. Alcohol and being in my feelings don't mix. Especially after almost six weeks of no drinking, while taking care of life's business. "Cute, younger than me, popular online, ain't doing shit, and full of shit. I feel so stupid. Stupid."

Tyra and Lily each grab one of my flailing hands to calm and reassure me that I'm not the only one who's fallen for style over substance in L.A. Carlos rolls his eyes and takes a sip of his drink, pinkie finger out like an auntie. He's seen and heard it all before during our fifteen years together as coworkers, classmates, and friends...my pattern, one he's pointed out many times, one that I know, but one that I just haven't broken.

"That's why I moved to New York after graduation," Tyra says. "Real Black men who don't play games. Too many people there to play games and miss out on a chance at love."

Lily, too, left L.A. for the San Francisco area shortly after our graduation for a new and higher-paying job and with a mission of finding a more educated and substantive Latinx man with similar credentials as she.

The challenge of being an educated professional of color in L.A. A bond that keeps Tyra, Lily, and me together any time they find a free weekend to come back to visit L.A. Carlos, luckily, remains in the L.A. area and attempts to keep in touch with me, although I don't accept too many of his and Ricky's invites—see, they still hang with my ex, and Ricky's bestie, DaVon.

While Carlos, Tyra, and Lily continue with small talk, I scroll and swipe anything and everything Brandon-Malik—his Instagram posts (nothing new since a week earlier, which I liked and probably shouldn't have), his IG stories (nothing new added today, but I rewatch last night's bowling night stories with unknown new friends), his followers (to see if anyone new is following him), then the IG activity timeline to see if he's liked any photos or followed anyone new in the past couple hours since texting me (nothing). Where is he and what is he doing now? Driving myself crazy. And I'm buzzed.

Carlos catches me. "Kenny, are you lurking on his social media again?"

"Um, no," I lie. Then go, "Yeah."

"Well, since you're on your phone, show me the breakup texts one more time," Tyra says and grabs my phone. "I need to see what this little nigga said again."

"Tyra and them trigger fingers," Lily says and laughs.

When I hand the phone to Tyra, I go, "Don't message him anything else."

It's both a plea and a call to action. It was Tyra's "hand me your phone" order one night in class that got Brandon-Malik to finally step up and take me seriously as a date, and moved us past the initial friend zone that we lingered in for weeks. The texts she sent on my behalf were a thousand times more forward and sexual than I'd initially felt comfortable sending to Brandon-Malik. As a practice, I generally move cautiously and slowly with men and life decisions. Obviously, not what my past six weeks have been with the spontaneous job resignation, selling my house, buying a new condo, and day drinking like I'm independently wealthy and don't need to start drumming up some consulting work.

Lily laughs. "Tyra's good at being the wing person. Until we find out the one she's pushing on us ain't shit."

We all chuckle again and bump fists as the server brings over another round of drinks for us. Despite the ninety-plus-degree weather, it feels light, airy, and free, with a bit of electricity with the Abbey's Drag Saturday performers nearby onstage. Or is it the drinks talking at three-something in the afternoon?

Tyra asks for the bill, as both she and Lily both have people to see, events to attend on their short weekend back in L.A. Carlos offers to stay behind and barhop with me if I'm game. I know he's game, Ricky's away. I'm game. No one and nothing to go home to.

"This is weak...his text," Tyra says. "Shitty way to break up with someone. What a fuckboy. You deserve better."

Lily chimes in, "Classic gaslighting and narcissistic behavior."

Carlos gives me that all-knowing look. Because he knows all. DaVon. Jeremy. Brandon-Malik. The other nameless ones who never made it past a first date or a first-night stand.

"Maybe part of it is me," I say and sip from what will be my fourth and final frosé of the afternoon. "I keep telling myself that maybe I could have reached out more when I was back home handling all the family stuff."

"Your mom died," Carlos, Tyra, and Lily say in unison.

"Or maybe I could have been more attentive in the months while finishing up the dissertation," I say, sounding like a pity party on what's supposed to be a fun Saturday afternoon reunion and drink fest with my former classmates. Not that I'm aiming for sympathy or anything. "Maybe I could have tried to be more...I don't know...I *am* eleven, twelve years older than Brandon-Malik, I'm not IG popular, I don't have an A-list crew...I hate feeling that I'm not enough, or wasn't enough, for him. I hate feeling like I'm not enough."

"Kenny, please," Carlos says. "Being busy with a dissertation and studying didn't break up Ricky and me."

"Fuck him," Lily says, "just like we said earlier. We're all doctors. We have substance. If someone doesn't see that, and they're stuck on superficial, that's on them."

"Kenny, chill," Tyra says. "Don't do this. You're Black. You're not even forty yet. You have a doctorate degree. You're fine. You care about people and social justice. You are a good catch."

I hear my friends, but I don't *hear* them. I don't know if it's the alcohol alone, the alcohol in combination with my feelings about everything happening in my life recently, or the alcohol and the summer heat. I know what Carlos, Tyra, and Lily are saying is true. At some point, I know, I will have to try and believe that what they are saying is true.

More work to be done.

Zaire

ICYF: Move

Another move. I've moved three times in two years. I'm a pro at this packing and going thing. I mostly leave or donate what I do not need. And I don't actually need much.

If you would have asked me a year ago, when I moved in with Mario, if I'd live in West Hollywood, I'd tell you, ab-so-lute-ly *not*, that white-ass city. But, as the old folks say, never say never, because here my Black ass is, in the heart of WeHo. I bet my housemate and I are the only Black*ish* people on this street or in a two-mile radius. I say Black*ish* because I don't quite know my housemate that well. I know he's Dominican, but I'm not sure if he identifies as Black, which clearly he is. We met on a moving and roommate app, as he had a room open, and after a few hours of chatting, I figured what the hell, give it a shot.

Thus, *aquí estoy*—here I am.

I've been in WeHo for about a month and a half. I do not *hate* it. Hell, I don't even actually *dislike* it. Minus the fact that it isn't a Black or Brown space, and this is a major minus, it's an *okay* city. I most enjoy the fact that I do not have to drive to the things I need or enjoy. I think I live on one of the few blocks where whole families reside. I've had a few notices on my door announcing property changes in the neighborhood. The few two-bedroom homes will be torn down, to make space for luxury apartments. I live in one of the oldest seven-unit apartments in the area. Thanks to rent control around here, I'm able to afford it all while getting a divorce. Lord knows I wouldn't be able to afford living in WeHo without my housemate's rent-controlled lease.

Some mornings, I wake up early and look out the front window, as we do not have curtains anywhere in our open-floor-plan dining and living room, and marvel at all the different family of trees and all of the greenery in my view. My favorite things to meditate over are the bush of bird-of-paradise flowers, the bundles of yellow angel trumpet flowers that align the fence near the front window, and the two Phoenix palm trees that cascade over our backyard near my bedroom window. The mini mansions that swirl through the Hollywood Hills aren't a bad sight either. Many mornings, I stare and take in these sightful joys. I've even noticed a Black guy jogging around the neighborhood in the early morning. I think he lives on this street. I don't think he's Black-Black, though. I do not know any actual brown-skinned Black men running or jogging in their neighborhoods wearing a hoodie. Not these days. Especially not since Trayvon. I for one do not jog/run in any neighborhood. That's what the track or my gym membership is for. He's probably one of them Black men that just *happens to be Black*, or of the Blaqué elite, comes from money, grew up around white people all his life. Wouldn't acknowledge the head nod if his life depended on it. Damn shame.

The question I'm centering this morning is if I should have some sort of friend gathering in my new place. The only ones to see my new place are the folks who helped me move in a few weeks ago. The rest only know of this move via my social media posts.

I must be making noise washing last night's dishes because my roommate has awakened and slowly saunters to the kitchen. He's never up before 11 a.m. Never.

"Morning, Zai," Alberto says. He is in his usual in-the-house get-up of gym shorts, ankle socks, and a bare chest. He's got one of those naturally built bodies that requires very little gym time, though he spends quite a few hours a day in the gym.

"Hey, Alberto," I say. "Good morning. Did I wake you with the dishes?"

"Nope. Just had to piss, and now I'm thirsty. What's with the pensive voice?"

I do not know Alberto that well yet, but from what I do know, he's quite observant. We do not even share that much space or time together. When I'm home, he's out working or enjoying L.A. But, when we cross paths, he seems to know how to read my energy. His sense of emotional intelligence is strong.

"How do you do that, Alberto?"

"Do what?" He stands next to me at the sink, lifting the filtered-water handle to pour himself a cup of water.

"Pick up on things. How did you hear in my 'good morning' that I was in deep thought?"

"Oh. I thought I told you, I'm a brujx." He laughs, then drinks the glass of water in three gulps. "I come from a long line of Black witches, voodoos, and healers on the island."

Oh, thank God he said Black. Because some of these obviously Black guys in WeHo refuse to say Black to describe themselves.

"Really?"

"Yes, really," he says. "You do, too, you probably just don't know it yet. But you will soon."

And like nothing, Alberto walks away, retreating back to his bedroom. I didn't get to tell him I was thinking about having folks over this weekend for a get-together.

"You should invite some of your friends over this weekend," Alberto yells from his room. "The space needs more of your energy!"

It's only been a month and a half living here, and I think for the first time in a long time, I've done something completely for myself. And it feels so right.

ZAIRE

ICYF: Work It Out

The office is frenetic and fast-paced throughout the week, so on Fridays it's pretty much a brunch fest. Last year I took a leap and changed career paths. I left my role at a university to be a diversity consultant for a very well-known social media company. Had I stayed in higher education during these trying-ass political times, I would have quit or been fired. The academy has much potential. It brought some joy being a lecturer and academic advisor supporting marginalized communities—Black and Brown students—navigate the ivory tower. But those joys never outweighed the whiteness of work, the constant competition of brilliance, and the performance of professionalism. The last straw for me—one day Harlem, my brother, texted me screaming about the white supremacist speaking live on my campus, and the campus president condoning the talk— the hate speech—as free speech. I knew then I had to leave working on a college campus.

I left my big solo office space for a shared circular cubicle-like space, and I enjoy it. It's more millennial, anyway. My work space sits in the middle of the room. All of the walls that aren't glass are colorful. My favorite wall is the orange wall of quotes by the community food quarter, also known in most places as the kitchen. The company is a nice place to hang out. There's two game rooms, a library, and on the rooftop there's a bar. The bar isn't the company's, but it's a perk of having the office in this building.

Upon being hired, all of the staff on our floor are asked to provide a quote that gets them through rough times and another one that makes them happy to read. All of the quotes are painted artistically on the wall and remain for as long as we work here.

I had gone to a private Frank Ocean jam session the night before I submitted my wall quote. Harlem got us access. He knew I had an infatuation with Frank. Everything Frank—his music, his look, his vibe. If I could build a partner, it would be someone like Frank. Around my age. Black. Creative. Tall. Sexy. Low-key. A Scorpio. I'm basically describing myself here, and I'm okay with that. I often tell myself, if I weren't me, and I knew me, I'd date me.

Anyway, I'm at the wall, reading the quote I added and contemplating if I should send the group text inviting the crew over to my new place for a weekend hangout. My quote is half of the short song "Good Guy" from Frank Ocean. It reminds me of my ex. It reminds me of how reserved I can be, how much more free I need to be…thanks, Frank.

"What you got planned for the weekend, Z?" Jada asks. Scared me, a bit, how she snuck up on me.

Jada is one of three Black people working on this floor with me. We jokingly call ourselves DC. Mixed work company thinks we call each other this because we come from DC, which we do not. DC is a reference to Destiny's Child. Jada, she claimed right away upon adopting the DC nickname, is Beyoncé. The rest of us haven't claimed Michelle or Kelly. Out of my colleagues, Jada feels like a bonus cousin of sort.

"I was just thinking about it," I say to her, then look back at the wall of quotes. "The weekend. I'm not sure yet."

"Well, I'm going to be in these streets this weekend," Jada says. "I'm talking about full throttle, no holding back. I saw Lamar's Insta post this morning talking about, *is the weekend ready for the heat I'm bringing?* I said boy, boo! He's a fuckboy, and I'm about to show his ass what ass he'll be missing."

I wasn't ready for all of that info. But that's Jada and I love her. Jada and Lamar are in this on-again, off-again shit*uationship*. We frequently talk about it. She mostly tells me about their drama and I add my two cents, which really isn't much. She usually knows what she wants to do anyway.

"You bettah be out there," I say and laugh. "Summer waits for no heaux!"

She throws a high five my way.

"You so right, Zaire!" Jada says. "Tonight, I'ma hit up Chris, my lil Tinder piece. He probably ain't doing shit, and have him take me to a dinner or something. There's this cute day party happening tomorrow in DTLA, you should come. You know us pushing-thirty gang loves us a day party and a brunch! Then on Sunday, if I don't go to church, the Black Brunch Gang is having a shindig, and that can be cute. So after I'm lit off those mimosas, I might sashay my ass to the Do-Over day party, and yes, you already know, you should come!"

I'm exhausted by Jada's run-on sentences and talking. But I take a mental note and catch all of the invites. I know I'll discard them. Jada is a good time. But, I can already tell, her weekend is about to be an Insta-frenzy. Posting every second, to make sure Lamar is watching. She's probably going to drink too much, and not really have that much fun, because she'll be focused on making sure it appears like she's having fun, which is work, and I do not have the energy for that this weekend. I like fun, but I'm also getting a divorce, and divorce is a mental trip. I haven't shared with Jada, or my other coworkers, about my divorce. They may not even know I'm married.

"Hey, Jada," I say, about to change the subject from partying and drinking the weekend away. "You know, you never told me which quote on this wall is yours."

"Are you sure you asked? I would have told you. You can probably guess it if you tried."

"There are over twenty quotes on this wall. I don't think I can guess it."

"Zaire," Jada says and places a hand on her right hip as to say I better know her quote.

"But I enjoy challenges. Don't tell me, let me try."

"Okay, boy. Try."

Jada walks to the free vending machine to get a mineral water.

I look over the quotes. Some of them are lyrics, like mine. Some are short poems. Others are parts of speeches and simple mantras. I try to do the process of elimination, figuring out the Black quotes. Majority are not. So, that leaves me with about five to seven. Jada is eclectic. She's a sistah, but one shouldn't be fooled with her diction, she's Ivy League educated and is the code switch duchess, so her quote is probably a reflection of her Black brilliance. I notice Audre Lorde, Zora Neale Hurston, and Janelle Monae. I'm almost certain it's Janelle.

"Okay, I'm halfway done with my water," Jada says, tapping her toe up and down on the wood floor. "Which is mine?"

"Well, I tried to do a process of elimination."

"I didn't ask about your method. Which is mine?" she cuts me off.

Damn Virgo.

"*I'm about women's empowerment. I'm about agency. I'm about being in control of your narrative and your body.* By Janelle Monae," I read out loud, a notch under being certain.

"You men sometimes," she says, "well, most times, don't pay enough attention."

She finishes her mineral water and places the glass in the recycle bin.

"Am I right, Jada?"

"That was a cute guess," she says. "You tried to hypothesize. You get a C for effort. My quote is a guy, who's on your team, and we share the same last name. And his first name is your last."

She glares at me like she's loving that I didn't know, but also hating that I didn't know.

"That was my second guess! James Baldwin! Duh! *You have to go the way your blood beats. If you don't live the only life you have, you won't live some other life, you won't live any life at all!*" I scramble to get out the quote in one breath.

When I finish saying the words, I realize I had never read those words on that wall before. This is my favorite part of working on this floor—besides DC. I had never read the words. Or maybe I do not remember. Life has a way of reintroducing things to you, when you need it, and it's as if you've never experienced it before. I feel at'ed, exposed. I begin to feel too much. *If you don't live the only life you have...you won't live any life at all.* FUCK.

"You's a lie and the truth ain't in you." She laughs. "What's with the face? You okay?"

"What face? I'm cool," I say. "Your quote—well, James Baldwin's quote—is a good one. You're at'ing me today." I try to lighten the moment on an already relaxed Friday. But these quotes can be a bit heady and intellectual.

"That's what I do best," Jada says. "Keeping you negroes in line. Anyway, I've been in the food quarter for too long with you. You joining me this weekend or what's up?"

"Nah. I was thinking about inviting folks over to my new spot tomorrow night. A small get-together. I was going to invite you, too."

"Ohhh, that can be fun," Jada says and pulls out her phone, slides a few fingers across the screen for whatever she's looking at. "Stop by your place for a bit and hang with the gurlzzzz. Your sexy brother Harlem, he on the invite list?"

"Obvi."

"Mmmkay. Let me know. I'm leaving work around two thirty, three o'clock. What time you headed out?"

"A little after three."

"Okay, well, keep me posted."

"Bet," I say as she walks away.

Divorce. I have to start living again. Living for myself. Tomorrow will be the start of a new journey, and I'm welcoming nothing but good vibes to my new home.

I look at the time. It's nearly 1:00 p.m. I send three group text messages. One to my siblings, one to my group with iPhones, and one to the Androiders (Lord bless 'em).

To: JamesGang
I've decided to show my appreciation to those who've
helped me get to where I'm at by inviting y'all to a

cute get-together at my new place. (Vannah, you can come too, even though you didn't help me pack or move *side-eye*). Tomorrow, Saturday, 7pm. Things to bring: good vibes. #issaNewBegining [emoji, emoji, emoji]

To: iPhones
Summer is still here.

I'm still queer.

And you heauxs need to see my new place.

Tomorrow, Saturday, 8:30 pm. Things to bring: good vibes & alcohol if you want. #issaParty #NoNewFriends [emoji, emoji, emoji]

To: Androids
Summer is still here. I'm still queer. And you heauxs need to see my new place. Tomorrow, Saturday, 8:30 pm. Things to bring: good vibes & alcohol if you want. #issaParty #NoNewFriends

As soon as I walk back to my desk, I receive messages.

JamesGang:
Vannah: Awww sorry big bro, I can't make it! I have plans. Can you start planning things ahead of time?!

Everyone dislikes Savannah's message.

JamesGang:
Langston: What a good lunch message to receive. Mark and I will be there.
Harlem: IssaParty! IssaParty! IssaParty! I might bring a plus one. Just fyi. See yall tomorrow. <3

I decide to check some emails and read some new articles I've got bookmarked about the wave of charter schools before I leave for the day. I recently learned about the charter school RISE, which aims to support youth with housing insecurity, or as it's known colloquially, youth who are homeless. That's innovative. With my job, I find it best to stay informed about innovative measures.

Mostly everyone checks out by three on Fridays. I tend to stay a little closer to four since I'm still new around here. Plus I live in WeHo, so my commute isn't that bad.

I spend a good hour reading articles. Then another few minutes on my social media, Twitter, Instagram, and I even stop to look at the grandparent of them all, Facebook. Then I open the text messages from my friends. All of them are excited about the party. I panic. I've made a plan to host people and I have not prepped or bought a thing. And I think about the fact that I have not hosted people in a long time. Not since…my old life.

I shut down all the electronic devices at work. I'm the last person on the floor. It is a few minutes shy of three p.m. I feel myself catching a wave of something. Maybe sadness. I do not know exactly why I am sad. I'm in a new place by my choice. Yet sometimes, I miss…

I do not finish that thought because it will not serve me well. Instead, I remember James Baldwin.

And head out the office.

KENNY

ICYF: Run Your Life

It's another Saturday evening and I have to get out of this house because I'm thinking too much.

Too much about my mom. Too much about loss. Too much about Brandon-Malik. Too much about being alone, especially after seeing and learning that Brandon-Malik has spent most of the day *not* alone, hiking the Malibu coast in the morning, pool partying at some hotel in downtown L.A., and pregaming with his roommates before a night out, most likely on the WeHo strip. And if I don't stop scrolling Brandon-Malik's social media stories and wondering what else and who else he's doing and why he hasn't contacted me since the *hi* text, I'm going to end up having one big pity party with myself.

Not that there's too much special about Brandon-Malik to be sitting up here by myself on a weekend evening. At least, that's what I tell myself—he's nothing special—to try and face reality that Brandon-Malik and I are no more. I've always been a sucker for a slides, socks, and shorts kinda man, what I call that perpetual basketball casual look. But there's only so much slides, socks, and shorts can do.

Once I hit thirty, I turned back the clock on my dating choices and went only for younger men. Now, months away from turning forty, I'm reconsidering a belief I've clung to—that younger men ask for so little, yet give so much. Definitely not in Brandon-Malik's case. When I stated I wanted more than a lot of good sex, good drinks, good dates, and good times—mostly at my expense, because I paid for everything, all the time—from Brandon-Malik, he was up front and steadfast in wanting no rules, no labels, no commitments with me. I stayed in it anyway. Convenient companionship, with me juggling work, doctoral classes, and everything else that comes with adulting.

I'm a mess. And I need therapy.

For most of the day, I've been working on presentations for the first few gigs I've lined up with my new consulting business. Got a community college's student life division training in Seattle next week, plus a workshop in Chicago for social workers who work with foster youth aspiring to higher education, and then a keynote address at a conference in Baltimore for scholars studying higher education and colleges. Keeping myself booked and busy in hopes of forgetting everything that weighs on my mind.

I skipped my morning workout and run through the neighborhood to get the work done for next week's gigs. The independence and freedom that comes with working for myself is something I love, but it comes with a price. Solo hours in my head. No one really to bounce ideas off of. Wanting to be around people, but also wanting to be alone. Thinking about how Brandon-Malik enjoyed sneaking in a quick study and work break to ease my tension. Wondering if the work I'm doing is current, given that I'm no longer in a school program nor working for an institution of higher education.

For many years I did diversity work at California University, East L.A., then left just after earning my doctorate and during "the funeral" period. Got an offer to become an associate vice president of student life at a local community college. Turned it down. When my mom died, I decided life's too short to be doing something for other people—or an institution—who aren't feeding me. Especially an organization that has the potential to take my energy, ideas, and creativity and nothing to offer in return but "give us more" and "what's next." I guess that's part of the territory of losing someone close, doing spontaneous things like calculating how long you can live on the insurance money you inherited, quit your profession, and go into business for yourself doing the same work an institution paid you to do, but on your own time and talent instead. Little did I know that weeks after losing my mom, Brandon-Malik would drop out of my life.

There is no manual for how to handle the loss of a parent. There is no instruction book for how to deal with the loss of a partner. The loss of both—within days, weeks, months of each other—I should be giving talks on the subjects of loss. Or at least incorporating loss and resilience themes into my upcoming work. Especially as a Black queer man. Maybe after some therapy—something I should have done almost ten years ago when the love of my life (at the time), Jeremy Lopez, got knifed in front of me and died. Yeah, that's next on the list of things to do. Therapy. Ten years too late. Not trying to go Kanye-cray with all these recent losses and transitions.

But for now, a run will do. Thinking three to five miles, whatever feels right while I'm out there in the West Hollywood streets. Thinking bright blue shorts, orange tank, gray shoes with the metallic emblems will work. Thinking I'll head north on my block to Santa Monica Boulevard, then west almost to the strip of bars, and then south on San Vicente until who knows where, and then circle back around eventually back to my block. See, I think too much. I should just let go and go where it feels right. Until I don't think about Brandon-Malik or my mom any more this evening.

I head out the front door and do some stretches near the row of planters adjacent to the curb. Even at dusk, the birds-of-paradise pop with color and vibrance. I've got the latest Beyoncé project blasting in my wireless headphones. I do a few jumps to warm up and notice a rideshare drop off a group of four male-appearing people. Cute. Laughing. Kiki'ing. Sipping outta Hydro Flasks. Looking like a cover of the "this is how to be in these streets when you're twenty-something and a queer person of color in West Hollywood" manual. One looking like Brandon-Malik so much that I'd be called a creeper if they saw the double and triple takes I'm making. Looks like they're headed to the new neighbor's place across the street.

The neighbor I've yet to meet. I guess this is the pregaming hour, like Brandon-Malik and friends were doing online, before people make their way over to Trunks, Fiesta, Blow, blah blah blah tonight.

So much for a riveting Saturday evening. I'm going running instead.

ZAIRE

ICYF: They Be Watchin'

Sunday. I'm barely getting out of the shower when I hear my doorbell ring. This is weird. It's noon and I'm not expecting anyone, especially after last night's gathering at my place. Alberto, my roommate, didn't come home last night after many of us caravanned over to the clubs. I almost leave whoever it is at the door because I'm hungover, despite the shower, and I do not want to interact with anyone today. Last night wore me out. Memo to self: Never accept drinks from Jordan again.

The doorbell rings again.

"Open the door," a familiar voice says. "Now!"

"I'm coming!" I wrap a towel around my wet body and walk to the front door. My living room still has empty cups from last night's pregame.

I open the door and there stands my sister Savannah.

"Savannah! What are you doing here?"

She is gorgeous. I haven't seen her in months. She's the sibling who dodges my invitations. I used to think it was because I'm queer. I've later come to realize that that isn't the issue, because her best friend is a lesbian. I think the issue is with me. She's let her hair grow and it's much longer than the last time I saw her. Her skin is radiant. She's always had good skin, but hunny is glowing, looking like an Instagram filter.

"Happy Sunday to you too," she says, rushing past me. "Sorry to push you, I have to use your restroom. Where is it again?"

"Down the hall, third door on the left." Again? As if she's been to my new apartment since I left Mario. Well, I'll be damned. Out of all the people to show up unannounced, I wasn't expecting my sister Savannah. Her life is usually planned and regimented, because Miss Thing is a special events coordinator for CBS.

"Ohhhhhhhh. Thank you, sweet Jesus!" Savannah exclaims from the bathroom, door ajar. I can hear her clearly. Too clearly.

"What are you doing here?" I yell from my bedroom, while also searching for clean underwear to put on. A towel around my waist and a bare torso…not the way to greet my sister.

"Hold on, Zaire, let me wash my hands."

My house isn't dirty, but it's just not that clean either. The pile of dirty clothes near the laundry hamper is two weeks high. If Savannah comes into this room, I know she'll make an unpleasant comment and I'd have to return the pettiness. My energy level is already low from last night. I sniff-test some briefs, throw on some running shorts over them, and a T-shirt, and close the bedroom door behind me. Savannah's waiting in the hall just outside my room.

"You're not going to show me your room?"

"Had I known you were coming, I would have straightened up a little," I say. "My sex gadgets are all over the room, I know you don't want to see that." I figure that's a way to gross her out a bit.

Savannah squints her eyes and glares at me. "You're right. I'll pass."

We walk to the living room and into the kitchen. I'm dehydrated.

"Want something to drink? I have water, lemonade, and whiskey?" I ask. "And this is my last time asking, what brings you over? How did you even get in? You've never been here."

"You look like you need some water," she says. She pauses and looks at me. "Looking like you've been rode hard and put away wet."

I look at her. We look at each other.

I pour a cup of water without taking my eyes off her. And she doesn't bat an eye. She and I are alike in ways she wouldn't admit. Out of the four James siblings, we are the most stubborn.

Then she continues, "We're here to take you to lunch."

"We?"

"Langston is in the car waiting for us to come down," Savannah says. "We couldn't find parking, so she decided to just stay in the car. So, I'm going to need you to hurry up and drink your water, then put some shoes on so we can take you to lunch."

She is talking faster than usual. She's always been a super-fast taker. But this is too fast for even her Speedy Gonzales ass. Something is up, and I do not have the energy to figure out whose mess in the James family I'm going to have to help clean up this time.

"Well, I do need to eat," I say. "Why the surprise pop-up? How did you know I didn't have company?"

"First of all," Savannah says and rolls her eyes. "One, I saw your 4:37 a.m. video post, saying thank goodness you made it to your bed. You wouldn't make a video like that if you had company over with you. Two, calm down and hurry up, our reservation is at one and I don't want to be late. Three, are you going dressed like that?"

Well, I've been told.

We—the JamesGang—don't talk much during the drive. I sit in the back with my shades on. I ask my sisters to lower the music and turn up the air-conditioning. Langston is driving. Savannah is the DJ. We are listening to gospel because it's Sunday. I do not mind it. I miss good gospel music. I haven't gone to church in years, since our parents used to force us at least twice a month. I close my eyes and listen to Langston humming the lyrics of "Made a Way."

I fall asleep. Well, doze off. Praying this headache goes away.

When I wake up, we are parked and Langston is looking back at me smiling.

"Good morning," Langston says. "We are here."

Langston is the sweet sister, but don't piss her off, because then she's the very mean one.

If I wasn't already skeptical about this surprise lunch, bringing me here would definitely raise my curiosity. But I'll continue to play it cool. I will not ask any questions, I'll see where this goes.

When we sit, no one is talking. They know I'm on to something. Not only are we at La Louisanne, but we have magically been seated at our usual family table. These heifers must think I'm boo-boo-the-fool.

"This is a nice touch," I say to break the silence. "Our table."

"See, Vannah, I thought he'd appreciate being at this table," Langston says, trying to be light in speech and energy.

"He's being sarcastic, sweetie," Savannah says in her *I'm-not-stupid-bitch* pitch. I taught her how to talk that way.

Our server arrives and asks for our drink requests. I order us all Muddy Waters—lemonade and iced tea—and a round of mimosas.

"I'll have the brunch bottomless mimosas," Harlem says, surprising us all as he arrives behind the server.

If Harlem is here now, I know I'm out of the loop. Something is up.

"I'll have bottomless too, then," I say to the server before they walk away. I could be paranoid or annoyed, but I think I hear Savannah smack her teeth at my order change. She's such a stickler for consistency. When we order our food, we shouldn't change it, in her eyes.

"It took you long enough," Langston says to Harlem as he goes around and gives us all a hug and a kiss on the cheek.

Langston, Harlem, and I start our first mimosa, while Savannah hasn't touched hers yet.

"So what's the tea?" I say, hoping somebody will just spill it and explain to me what the hell is going on.

I know this isn't a regular JamesGang Brunch. Had it been a regular brunch, I would have been in the loop from the beginning. Savannah would have told me days before. She isn't one for surprises. Then it hits me. She's pregnant. I think my sister is pregnant.

I look over at her again to be sure I'm not tripping. I go over the clues. She hasn't touched her mimosa. Now, I know I can drink, but Ms. Black Sorority beats me when she's throwing back libations. She can drink like a fish. Savannah's skin is glowing, her hair is healthy, and now that I'm looking, she's gained a little weight, nothing too drastic of a change for someone who isn't skilled like I am skilled to see people. Before I am about to blurt out my epiphany, Harlem clears his throat.

"Well, just so we are all very clear," Harlem says, "I was invited by Vannah and Langst, and you all know I have a hard time skipping out on free food and mediocre company."

Harlem thinks he's funny with that dig, *mediocre company*. But he isn't lying about him enjoying free food. Savannah and I usually always pay for our family outings, being the oldest two JamesGang siblings. We used to fuss about who's paying. Since the passing of our mother, I've always felt it was my responsibility to pay for them, but Savannah always wants to help or at minimum pay her portion. So we often go back and forth—*I have it. No, I have it. Let me pay half. Just get the next one*, blah blah—but ever since apps like Venmo, ApplePay, and Cash App have entered our lives, we do not go back and forth. If I pay the bill I'll be sure to have funds in one of my accounts from Savannah, and vice versa.

Then Langston chimes in, "Vannah organized this brunch, and I'm with Harlem, free food and *the best company* is always a nice touch to Sundays."

She's sweet.

I look over to Savannah, who is on my right and makes herself the head of the table. I can see right through her fake calmness. Although I do not like surprises, I am actually thrilled at the idea of our family expanding. I'm going to be an uncle! I see her parting her lips to speak, but I jump in.

"Savannah, it's okay, you do not have to be nervous," I say. "I know why we are here together, at our special booth."

"You do, Zaire?" all my siblings say in unison.

"It's very little you all can get past me," I say. I look around the booth. They are all puzzled. Harlem is looking at Langston, Langston looking at Savannah, and Savannah looking at Harlem. "Savannah, although you and I do the least amount of talking amongst the four of us, I'm still your brother and I'm here for you."

"Excuse me?" Savannah says.

"I know you're pregnant," I say as I sip the last sip of my mimosa.

Langston and Harlem gasp.

"What, I'm going to be an auntie?" Langston squeals.

"Wait a minute. No! Yes. I mean, maybe! But, wait, how did you know?" Savannah speeds out her mouth.

Harlem waves down the server to request more rounds of mimosas while also chugging the mimosa pregnant Savannah hasn't touched.

"I pay attention to details," I answer, excited that I've figured out why we are all here together for this impromptu brunch.

"Well, yes, I'm pregnant," Savannah says. She is slow and pointed in her speech. She seems scared. I realize that perhaps this wasn't the time to be the winner at the game Clue. "But I was *not* planning on sharing with anyone yet. It's too early to share. I'm almost three months, and it's advised to keep pregnancy low-key until after the first trimester. I don't want to jinx it."

The server refills our drinks. Harlem chugs. I chug. Before the server leaves, we have another full glass.

"Your food will be out shortly," the server says.

"We haven't ordered," I say.

Savannah shoos her hands at us. "Everything was pre-*ordered*."

I look at the table and realize there are no menus here, and ask who made the orders and what are they having me eat.

"Zaire, I ordered for everyone," Savannah continues. "I arranged this brunch. The reason I called us together is. Because. We feel…"

Langston clears her throat and reminds Savannah to use *I* statements. Using *I* statements when we had family discussions was a communication skill our mother encouraged us to uphold. We were rarely allowed to speak on behalf of anyone else. We had to say "I feel that…, I think this…," not "*we* feel that…, *we* think…," and if anyone else felt that way we'd add, "I feel that way too, I think that as well." It's a practice I carry in my personal life. *I* statements allow us to speak more honestly about our personal thoughts and feelings. Plus it keeps us away from generalizing others.

Savannah hesitantly continues, "*I* feel. You may have. A. Drinking problem."

Harlem chugs his drink and the food arrives. Everyone is having their own specialized combination of Louisiana-style shrimp & grits with a side of biscuits.

I begin to laugh.

I begin to laugh hard.

This is a joke. *A drinking problem.*

I scan the table, but no one is laughing. There aren't any smirks. This is serious. I slowly collect my laughs and stare at them. I ask who else thinks this way. I know they must have other thoughts, because I know they must not really believe I have a damn drinking damn muthafucking problem.

Langston shares her thoughts, and at this point I'm staring at them like a blank canvas. A blank face.

"I don't think you have a drinking problem," Langston says. "However, I do think you're drinking more than you used to. I admit when Vannah brought it up to me a few weeks ago, I hadn't noticed. But then I started to notice you drinking much more than what I was used to seeing you drinking."

"And how do you all know I'm drinking more?" I ask. "You're not actually with me all the time. Hell, most of you have only been to my new place twice since I announced my divorce plans."

I need receipts.

"You post every damn thing these days," Savannah goes. "I watch all of your stories on social media. And five times out of the week, you're out at some bar with some friend. Or at some function with some friend. And you're usually inebriated."

Savannah speeds all this out her mouth in record time.

Receipt valid.

I nod and look over to Harlem. I know out of the group, Harlem is going to help me out here. He leans in and he gets a bit serious, and before he opens his mouth, I know I've lost this battle. They think I'm an alcoholic.

"Listen, big bro, I love you," Harlem goes. "You're my favorite brother."

"I'm your only brother," I interrupt. "Harlem, now get to it."

"Well, basically, I do not think you're an alcoholic," Harlem goes. "But I do feel like you're drinking daily, and not a glass of wine kind of drinking. You're going ham, even for someone like myself. So, I think you're masking your shit, and although we talk daily, you do not really *talk*-talk to me, not about the things that got you drinking…"

"Like Mario," Savannah says and starts eating her food. She did not even wait for anyone to mention grace. She's hungry with her pregnant ass.

The rest of brunch has all the makings to be awkward. The three of them, the JamesGang, gang up on me, call me an alcoholic, and encourage me to be a fuckboy instead of drinking so much. Langston, with her Christian saint ass, even says while I'm going through this divorce, being a fuckboy is valid and okay. I don't know where that psychology comes from—to fuck around instead of drinking, but then again, no one in the JamesGang is a counselor, therapist, psychologist, or psychiatrist. Thank God the food is good.

Regardless of the occasion—an intervention—it is always refreshing to be around my siblings. They can be quite dramatic, especially that Savannah, but they care deeply.

I know I do not have a drinking problem. I am just sad and getting familiar to this new life without Mario. It is nice to know there are people who are watching from a distance and wishing the best for me. Brunch isn't what I expect today, and yet it is full of what I needed. A reality check. And a reminder that I need to stop posting so much on my social media. Or that I need to block some people from watching my online life.

Caring or not, some people are nosy and make shit up in their heads. That's the JamesGang for you.

KENNY

ICYF: Notice the Patterns

So the thing about me is this. I am in my feelings all the time. Someone gives me the eye, or a smile, or laughs at one of my dry-humored jokes, remotely gives me some attention...and I'm head over heels, heels over head. Literally. I fall hard, fast, and ugly. I fall for the wrong people. I fall for people with problems. People who need fixing. Or who I perceive need fixing. Or who need me. Or who I want to need me. I want to be needed. Yeah, that's a pattern. I know my patterns. I've just never done anything about them...until now.

I've fallen in love three times that are significant—*really* significant—in my life. The other times I've fallen in love...well, I was just lovestruck, and looking back, I really didn't like them at all. Looking back gives you some perspective, for sure. All those so-called potentials with nothing but good looks, an attentive dick, and potential. Show me potential—or what I *think* is potential—and it's on.

The first was DaVon Holloway, this firefighter/EMT type I met through my best friend Carlos. Carlos's partner, Ricky, and DaVon were and still are best friends. So hanging with Carlos can be complicated sometimes, you know, because I can't say too much about who I'm seeing or fucking around with because I don't want it getting back to DaVon, who's happily married to his second wife and raising a little Mr. and Mrs. Black America family in the suburbs. Oh yeah, DaVon is bisexual, had a habit of stepping out on me with other men and women, but had one of those quiet sexy auras that kept me "forgetting," forgiving, and finding my way back into his life. I'm a sucker for tall, dark-skinned Black men. And if they're a working professional? Lordt.

DaVon and I did a good six years together. Lived together. Moved to our own separate places. Lived together again. Broke up. My mom, who lived with me at the time, had mixed feelings about DaVon...as most mothers probably do, when they see their own patterns repeating in their children. Anyway, you identify a relationship stage in a textbook, and DaVon and I exemplified it. I wanted our own little Black American Dream, until I finally let the dream—and DaVon—go.

The second one, his name was Jeremy Lopez, *that* was complicated. And unexpected. We were complete opposites in every way you can think of. I had a master's degree. He was going to East L.A. Junior College. I was barely thirty. He had just turned twenty-one. I'm Midwestern Black with Southern roots. And Jeremy was Afro-Latino, from Mexican and Dominican roots. I was conventional and a bit straitlaced, a nerd at the time. Jeremy had a spontaneous I-don't-give-a-fuck energy that comes when you're twenty-one, new on the gay scene, and know you look good. I knew that I didn't need to be with someone like Jeremy, someone who had nothing to offer but good—and I mean *good*—sex all day, every day whenever I could get away from my work. His family was complicated and huge and poor in terms of money. Mine was simple—at the time—my mom had moved out to California from Ohio to live with me after separating from her then-husband. I owned a small house in Monterey Park, bought when regular people could kinda buy houses in the L.A. area, had a nice, newish BMW truck, and could take care of myself.

I kept myself above reproach and never got into any kind of trouble—like with the law. But Jeremy had brothers who kept getting into trouble and kept him on the verge of trouble. I was a one-person-relationship kind of person, much like I was with DaVon.

Jeremy... Well, let's just say that Jeremy was popular. And new on the scene. And had the whole height, six-pack, and smile, and...dick. And did I say he was twenty-one? And did I say dick? And twenty-one-year-olds are not about that one-person life. And we did the back-and-forth, break-up, make-up thing more than enough times. And when we were gonna try...again...for like the two-hundredth time, Jeremy was stabbed—mistaken identity for his brother—and died in my arms. Blood on the ground, on our clothes, he died right in my arms. We were so close to having our happy ending, and never had a chance. We just never had a chance from the start.

So I stayed off the market for a long time. A *long* time after Jeremy Lopez died. Like seven years *long* time. My mom eventually moved back to Ohio to live her single, divorced, senior citizen life. And I just dove into work. That's about it. The good part is that I worked with my best friend, Carlos, at the same campus, so we just had this good synergy going and I didn't realize that I was a workaholic going nowhere fast. I started focusing on my fitness—mostly for superficial reasons, definitely not for health—and if I wasn't at work, I was running around the neighborhood or working out at my local gym. And that's where Brandon-Malik came into the picture.

You know that whole saying about it hits you when you least expect it? So, like, when I'm running or working out, I'm in a zone. I'm focused on technique, reps, weight, and time. And improving. I'm not one of those socialites at the gym or track. But one day, at my gym, I started noticing this new guy coming in at the five a.m. shift—people like me working out before our workdays start. Some mornings, he'd play basketball. Some mornings, he'd do the StairMaster. Most, he did free weights, which was not my area of the gym—I'm a machine weights kinda guy.

It just started as a *hmmm.*

Hmmm...that he was Black and in my part of town, because there weren't a lot of us living east of downtown L.A.

Hmmm...that he was kinda hot in his socks, slides, and shorts as he sidled slowly into the gym.

Hmmm...that he played basketball at the outdoor courts adjacent to the track I ran on in the mornings or on weekends.

Hmmm…that he and I had similar items in our grocery carts when we happened to be at Trader Joe's at the same time.

Hmmm…when, after one of those three-day weekends when you don't have to work on Mondays, and you drink yourself into oblivion, and you post a million stories on social media tagging yourself in almost every bar in #WeHo with a million #BlaQueer #BlackBoyJoy #BlackAndBae hashtags, and he slides into the DMs after scrolling through said hashtags a few days later, and goes, "You're from my gym. That's what's up. Get at me sometimes. Let's link up," and so you decide to Get.At.Him and Link.Up, because DMs are new to you, especially DMs from a blogger/stylist/fitness/coach who has 15k followers and only follows 198 pages, and then all of a sudden you have a Kenny and Brandon-Malik thing going on. Or so you think.

I'm sitting in the driveway of my condo and thinking about how grateful I am to have found Naija, a Black queer woman, to share therapy time and billable hours with. Feeling a little bit guilty that my first session was all about men and relationships and not one thing about my mother, my recent academic and professional achievements, nor my angst of having given up a pretty stable job and house in the suburbs to live in this not-so-Black-friendly place called West Hollywood. That's so indicative of my life. Chasing men and relationships. Neglecting everything and everyone else. But still just grinding through succeeding without any balance, without being in the moment and realizing what's in front of me that I'm neglecting. Damn. That's an aha moment.

Le Sigh. Sunglasses on. Getting out the car.

I see my young Black neighbors from across the street walking up to their rental apartment building with a couple Whole Foods canvas bag in tow. They're kiki'ing up a storm, like homie-roomie-friends ought to. I see the tall one—who looks somewhat intellectual, with his swimmer-body, brown-skinned self—rocking short, natural curls. The other one—I call him Little Miss Hot Pants—is always wearing some short shorts, shirtless (like today…on a grocery store run!), and always meeting/greeting some new trick at their building's front gate. We've never talked, nor do they look my way now, though I do like checking out what's going on in their lives through my upstairs living room window. So nosy. And so West Hollywood. Only "Black" Black guys talk to each other, when we all should be allies with each other given the anti-Black world that we live in.

But that, my dears, is something for another therapy session.

KENNY

ICYF: Revisit Your Past

"So how was the Seattle gig? How was therapy? Have you heard from Brandon-Malik again?"

Carlos is rat-a-tat-tat with the questions this evening, barely giving me time to get my napkin out the holder and onto my lap. We're meeting up at Bossa Nova, a longtime and reliable food spot on Robertson, just across from the Abbey. On the plane back from the East Coast, I was craving one of their quinoa salads—minus the gorgonzola; meatless and vegan Monday, you know. That's what I told Carlos when he asked where we should meet up. What I didn't tell Carlos is that one of Brandon-Malik's roommates works as a server at the restaurant, and I was hoping that if he saw me or served our table, he'd take notice and text or DM Brandon-Malik.

"One question at a time, Carlos, geez," I say, hoping I don't sound impatient with Carlos but knowing I probably am.

"Sorry about that, Kenny," he says. "We have a lot to catch up on."

"No, I apologize. I know I can be snappy and impatient when I'm hungry."

"And horny," Carlos says. We laugh. "Have you gotten any recently? Since Brandon-Malik? I hope that's not being too intrusive."

"It's not," I say. "And no, I haven't. I know...*the ghetto*. But not in a space, place for that energy quite yet."

"It's soon, true-ish, but sex positivity and all, needs have to be met," he says and we nod in acknowledgment of desire fulfillment. "So one thing at a time. How were your presentations?"

"Well, first I made almost fifteen grand from the three gigs—Seattle, Chicago, and DC," I say and pour a glass of wine from the bottle Carlos has already had a head start on. "Not bad for a week and a half of work."

"Better than student affairs, that's for sure."

"Made some great contacts, but we'll see how that pans out," I say. "Hard trying to start a new business."

"You're welcome back at CUELA, if it fits."

"Nope, not doing that," I say. "I like the independence for now."

"Sounds like a better fit for you than being at an institution."

"For sure," I say. "Though the white-woman tears and liberal white racism are still the same, whether it's at my events or on a campus. Can't escape them tears."

"Oh Lordt," Carlos says and rubs his thumb and pointing finger together. And simultaneously, we both go, with a laugh, "World's smallest violin."

My mom's favorite saying. Memories. That I don't want to get into right now. The littlest thing takes me to my feelings.

There's an awkward silence between us. The air is thick with us both thinking about my mom's death. She knew and liked Carlos a lot. Ricky, Carlos's partner, too.

"Sorry," Carlos says.

"Hey, it's bound to happen," I go. "I can't just pretend like she's not dead."

"We can talk about something else…"

Carlos is uncomfortable, I can tell. Though we're best friends, no one wants to be talking death and dying all the time they're around me. Not on a random weekday night in WeHo, over dinner and wine. So I go, "Sure…"

Carlos takes the out.

"Ricky and I are in escrow on a place in Palm Springs. We should have it ready for Labor Day weekend. Not a lot of work to be done."

"Awww, how exciting." I sip, well, gulp the wine, which tastes sweet and tasty like Kool-Aid, but it's not Kool-Aid. "It's about time. Hashtag goals."

"And we'll have some of Ricky's gays from the hospital out there," Carlos says. "Maybe we'll finally get you married off to a doctor."

"I *am* a doctor."

"Oh, I remember. We both are."

"Oop," we say and clink our glasses.

"Anyway, DaVon won't be invited to this shindig."

"Thanks, I would hope not," I say. "I'm sure his wife won't appreciate him being with his queer friends and ex over Labor Day, especially without her or the kids."

"Not our problem."

"Anyway, I'm not envisioning mingling with any exes anytime soon."

"Well, just Brandon-Malik, huh?"

"Well, now that you bring him up…" I say. But I'm saved by the food server and my quinoa salad and Carlos's salmon bowl. So L.A. Our menu. Our server is not Brandon-Malik's roommate. Nor does it look like Brandon-Malik's roommate is working tonight. Damn.

"What's up with Brandon-Malik, anyways? You heard anything? Since the *hi* text?"

I inhale and exhale. Poking around my salad with the fork. Disappointed I won't have a chance to maybe get on Brandon-Malik's radar tonight. Sad, once again, that Brandon-Malik continues to play this disappearing-act game.

I take out my phone. Get to Brandon-Malik's social media. He's got a red circle around his IG profile picture, indicating he has posted a new story. I hesitate at first, then watch his storyline. Ugh. Having drinks in downtown L.A. Crossed out the face of a guy he's drinking with, but tagged him. I open the tag to see Brandon-Malik's drinking partner tonight. A young, cute IG blogger with links to Cash Apps and OnlyFans, meaning he probably does porn. No judgment. Sex positivity. Still. I gave it up to Brandon-Malik in ways that would shame the ancestors. Back to Brandon-Malik's storyline, but now everything is deleted. That quick. I take a boring pic of my quinoa salad and wine glass, tag Bossa Nova, and hit send to my storyline. Just to show, well pretend, that I'm living, too. Will wait for an hour to see if he's watched my storyline. Ugh. Performance. I'm too old for this social media drama that's definitely not from my generation. That's my punishment for falling for another younger man. Naija the therapist would be disappointed, I'm sure.

"Um, Kenny?"

"Nothing. I haven't heard from him." I look up at Carlos and then down at my salad. Not feeling like eating now. Thinking about Brandon-Malik brings me down. The dumping part, more than the Brandon-Malik part. The that he's out there living in these streets part. The without me part. And then that mood that comes with mourning, where you go from happy to melancholy in seconds. "It sucks. Not hearing from him. Being ghosted. Still wondering why he gave up on me...on us, because of...you know."

"I'm sorry," Carlos says. "I really am. I know you've been through too much these past months..."

In my mind, I run through the script that I'll need to cover with my new therapist: a graduation, a funeral, a breakup, a resignation, and a move across town. I can't wait for Naija the therapist to help me make sense of these transitions.

"It's all right," I say and finally scoop a portion of salad onto my fork. I *was* craving it on the flight from the East Coast, after all. "You know what I just thought of? It's weird. Am I talking too much?"

"You're hardly talking at all." Carlos goes and pours both of us another glass of wine. "What's up?"

"I'm sorry if I'm rambling so much about nothing," I say and take a sip. "But everyone leaves me. DaVon, Jeremy, Brandon-Malik...my dad and my mom. I've never left anyone. I'm a loyal one."

"I don't know what to say about that."

"You don't have to say anything," I say. "And then I just remembered that Jeremy's birthday is coming up in a few days.

Can't believe that little twenty-one-year-old kid from East L.A. would be thirty now. Like that's real adult status."

"Time flies."

"Too fast," I say. "I wonder a lot about what he'd be doing now. His potential finally realized? If we'd have made a go of it again—for the fifth time—if Jeremy hadn't died?"

"That's dramatic, Kenny."

"Well, is this?" I ask. "I think I'ma go see him on his birthday."

Carlos looks up from his salmon bowl and stares at me like I'm losing it.

"Not see him, see him," I say. "But go out to the cemetery. Talk to him a bit."

"When was the last time you've been there?" Carlos asks.

I pause, trying to remember but knowing I haven't gone since the service.

"Well, the funeral." Nine years ago, however, I don't say out loud.

"What?" Carlos shifts uncomfortably in his seat, his mouth agape. I think I've shocked him with the news that I've not been to Jeremy's site…ever. "That's a long time. You feel okay about that, Kenny?"

"I'm cool," I say. "Actually Naija, my therapist, suggested that since I seem to have a pattern of feeling being left, that I think about initiating closure with the people I didn't have it with."

"Homework? In a way?"

"Yeah. Something like that. What better time than Jeremy's thirtieth to have a few words?"

"As long as you think you can handle it, best friend, I'm all for it."

Without hesitation, I hold up my wine glass, motion for Carlos's glass, and go, "I'll drink to that."

ZAIRE

ICYF: They Come Back

Here I am trying to enjoy Wednesday evening after work, alone in my living room, with whiskey and Netflix. Relaxing. Alberto, my roommate, is gone all week, taking care of his mother in New Jersey. She's having open heart surgery in a few days. I swear sometimes life feels like parties and funerals.

I shouldn't be thinking about his mother's death. Besides her failing heart, she's pretty healthy from what Alberto shares. But from my life's experience, once you go in to the hospital for one thing, you'll leave with three more. Or, you don't leave. That's trauma talking. That's Black life talking. That's me skipping out on therapy for three years talking. I'm just talking. His mother isn't dying. She isn't going to die. She's just having open heart surgery. Like mine did nine years ago this week and never came home. Alberto mom's story isn't my mom's story. I am just talking.

At 8 p.m. every night, my phone goes to Do Not Disturb mode. I started doing that a couple of years ago when Mario, my ex, and I started to become more known in the LGBTQIA community, thanks to Mario's connections with the promoters and party planners in the QTPOC in crowds. We became a *subculture mini famous couple.* I didn't like the attention; I did, however enjoy access to private parties. VIP sections and the run of party favors weren't my favorite, but I have been known to go and flow with it. Do Not Disturb was my way of making sure Mario and I had some sense of separateness from the world. Now it's personal wellness.

I'm on my second whiskey on the rocks and two episodes into some weird-ass animated show that I probably should be watching while high off weed, when my phone rings. I'm puzzled because it's an hour past Do Not Disturb. I turn my phone over, and to my complete surprise it's Mario. My ex. Calling me. We haven't spoken in months. I am hesitant to answer the phone. I know I only have two more rings before it goes to voicemail. Guilt from I do not know where starts to seep in real quick. I start to sweat.

I answer.

Of fucking course.

I always answer.

I always reply.

I am always there—for Mario.

"Hello?" I'm trying to sound cool, calm, and collected. There isn't a response, so I repeat it, a bit more confident, hoping this was a butt-dial. "Helloooo."

"Yes, I hear you," Mario says. These are the first words I hear from Mario in two months.

"Did you mean to call me?" I do not know what else to say.

"I did." He isn't being petty here. He's searching for words. I hate this.

Silence. Another five seconds. Five seconds during an unannounced, unexpected, unwanted call from someone feels like too damn long to me.

"Okay," I say. "Well, since we aren't talking. I have to go check…"

I'm stuck trying to figuring out what I actually need to check, what can I say to get off this phone.

"Z, I'm trying to find the words to tell you," Mario says. "I know you do not like small talk, but I'm trying here, okay? So give me a second, damn it."

He's one of the few people who has learned how to loosen up my stubbornness.

"Okay, I figured you'd know what to say before you set yourself to call me," I say. "Perhaps a text will be better."

"I'm not as strong with my words as you are, Z," he says. "You know that." He rolls his eyes through the phone. I feel it, especially with the emphasis on the *t* when he says *that*. "I have all of these emotions this week. I know this isn't yours to carry, but I feel I need to tell you."

He is about to vent, I feel it. I do not know if I'm here for this tonight.

"Okay, so this is going to be a discussion?" I say.

I'm not so ready for a conversation. I get up from my sofa and walk to the kitchen. I look at the bottle of whiskey, think about pouring another drink, but I subconsciously feel my rehab team—my siblings—judging me. So I get a vegan ice cream sandwich out of the freezer instead. I figure it could cool me off because I feel my pressure rising from this conversation-to-be with my ex.

"This doesn't have to be a discussion," he says. "I just need to share with you two things. And I'll let you be booked and busy."

He's funny. Knowing damn well I'm not booked or busy. But he's right, I am over this talk already.

"I'm ready when you are," I say, gaining some kind of cockiness back.

He sighs, then says, "I was served Monday. A heads-up text would have been nice."

I filed for divorce. I told him I was. I didn't tell him when I did. I forgot. Okay, I didn't forget. I didn't want to have that conversation with him. These past few months I've tried to give space for him to share his thoughts, his feelings, and every single time, he's been short. Mean. Unbothered. So, I did what I had to do. I filed. I want to live my life free of any legal obligations. It's time for me to renew my passport and I do not want to select *married* on the application. I don't want to put *married* on any legal document anymore. I am single. I want to be single. I do not belong to anyone but myself.

"Would that be too much to ask for?" Mario continues. "A text would have sufficed. Do you know how that feels? How embarrassing? Having a stranger come to my home to serve me papers. Reminding me that the love of my life no longer wants to build with me. Monday was very hard for me. I know this isn't yours to carry. But I'm sharing because I do not know what else to do."

He is holding back tears. I feel it.

"I'm sorry, I didn't…"

"I'm not done, Zaire." Mario takes a deep breath. "I'm okay. I've survived Monday. The other thing that is on my heart today is…"

He takes another break. Five seconds. I get up from my sofa again. I go to the whiskey bottle. I pour another drink—my third tonight. Fuck my rehab team. What they do not know will not hurt them.

"Then today while getting my weekly pedicure, Marlena asked where have I been and asked about you," Mario continues. "You know, I've been really good at faking the shit these past couple months, but today I cried. I looked at my phone and I saw the date. And I know I forgot a lot of important shit in our relationship, like the time you planned a random middle-of-the-week lunch in our busy schedules, your way of trying to be romantic and I totally forgot to show up. I forgot so many things that were important to you, but one thing I made sure not to forget were significant dates like the one coming up. I know your mom's anniversary is this week."

At this point I am tipsy. Tipsy and feelings are like vinegar and oil, they do not mix. I'm regretting having my third pour. I'm also regretting answering this phone call. I could have let it go to voicemail and never listened to said voicemail. But I answered, and here I am. I need to end this call quick fast and in a hurry before the dam of tears breaks. Emotions.

"Mario, I'm sorry I didn't give you a heads-up about filing for the divorce," I say. "You are right, a heads-up text would have lessened the blow. However, it's pretty late and I have an early meeting, so—"

"Thanks for answering," Mario interrupts me. "I didn't think you would. I just want to know if you're taking care of yourself. Every year around this time you seem to float around. I don't know who you're with these days and I don't know—"

"I'm fine," I cut Mario off.

I do not want this conversation. Who I'm with or not with these days isn't for him to know. Plus, we shouldn't be sharing feelings anymore. We're divorcing. One thing could lead to another…and I'm not going back there—with Mario—anymore.

"That's what you say," Mario says. "But are—"

"I'm fine," I say. "I'm going to go to bed. Thanks for caring. Now. Goodbye."

I manage to get this out. I hang up the phone and I weep.

I wake up at 3:37 in the middle of the night. I must have wept myself to sleep on this sofa. I haven't had a cry this way in a long while. The first thing I do before I get my ass up from this sofa is remove Mario's contact from my Favorites. I remember that's the only way he was able to call me direct even with my Do Not Disturb. I cannot afford another unannounced call.

Zaire

ICYF: There Is a Beginning

It's really not all that juicy. He didn't cheat. I didn't cheat, unless you count the times I thought about having sex with someone else in my head. We didn't fight or argue often. He didn't have bad breath or smelly feet. We just grew apart. This may sound extremely basic but it's the damn truth. People change. I changed. The things I was once interested in, I am no longer into. The things that brought us joy as a couple do not entertain me any longer.

Mario was a sceney-socialite who came from a Black elite background. A long line of debutantes, Black Greeks, and light-skinned money. His family migrated from the South in the early 1940s and settled in the hills of Los Angeles. These things intrigued me when we first started off, but as the years went by, I became less and less enamored with what we had.

From the outside looking in, we were on our way to becoming Mr. & Mr. BlaQ Los Angeles Elite. Mario had us on all the party lists, private dinners, and A-list gatherings, all Black, both queer and straight. For the first three years we were together, we'd go on vacation every season and we'd have connections—his connections—in every city. I loved the access, I loved how Mario wooed people. His smile was easy to fall for. His *aire of carefree* was attractive. It's what allured me to him.

Our weekends were rarely empty. Always a full schedule. Being from a lineage of light-skinned money and debutantes, activity ensues. There was always someone's dinner, someone's wedding, someone's whatever celebration. If not a family member, then a close friend of the family. In between what I call performance activities—show up, smile, small talk, talk about your last trip somewhere, your upcoming trip or charity, overdrink but never *never* let it show that you're drunk, all performance—there was little time for us to be us. The first three years of our partnership I did the performance well. It was fun. I felt fortunate to be invited into a whole new world. A Black puff puff world. I was used to middle-class money. White middle class. Not Whitley Gilbert meets Dwayne Wayne. Then around year four, I couldn't take another charity dinner. Didn't feel interested in So-and-So's travel noir trip to—insert European country here, because his Black elite crew never did the continent of Africa. I couldn't take it anymore, plus it was getting too expensive.

I don't come from money like that. I don't have the security blanket of family support. Mario has his successful parents. His dad, Maurice, is still one of my favorite people of all time. He is a pediatrician. His sweet and intense mom, Maria, is an accountant, a partner in a firm she co-owns. So homeboy didn't have to worry too much about finances.

❖

Mario and I met at our mutual friend Jordan's house party. I was twenty-three, finishing up my last year in grad school, and Jordan was in his first year of grad school. I didn't do much partying in grad school, it was all work, work, work, drink, drink, paper, paper, drink, drink, work, work. And if I was lucky I'd have sex a couple times a month. Jordan and I had become friends through a student organization that aimed to connect men of color, called Brother Connection. The organization was made up of majority Greek-letter-affiliated dudes. Jordan was a Greek. The only pledging I did was BAK, Beta Alpha Kappa, otherwise known as Beyoncé Alpha Knowles. We connected over our like of BAK and we were some of the few graduate scholars in the organization, so we became honorary advisors. One Friday, Jordan's family left for Valentine's Day weekend and he decided to have a party at the family house. It was a Red, Yellow, Green party. Every attendee had to place a colored-coordinated button on their shirt indicating their relationship status. Red meant taken/coupled. Yellow meant complicated or open, you had to ask. Green meant single.

I arrived late to the party. Almost didn't go because—papers. I wore nothing special, nicely fitted blue jeans and a gray T-shirt with my school's name on it—the University of Spoiled Children. Jordan's parents' place was near Mario's family house, I would find this out that night. Jordan and Mario are childhood friends and fraternity brothers. I would find that out that night as well.

I walked up the long, beautifully-lit-and-landscaped path toward the door, nervous as hell. *Am I really going to a Stop-and-Go party? Do people actually participate?* I get a step from the door and my hands are a bit clammy, the door opens, and it's Jordan greeting me. He had read my text letting him know I was near, right on time.

"My main man, you made it!" Jordan says and gives me the Black man handshake hug.

"Of course, I told you I would be here," I say, knowing damn well I almost didn't come.

"Here, I got you the green button to put on your shirt," Jordan says, placing it directly over my left chest. "I know your ass is single. I see you've been working out them pecs!"

He brings me inside. The party is full of shades of Brown-skinned people, mostly men. Drooling. I already know I will need a bucket. In the living room sits a grand piano with a giant white polar bear rug underneath it. Most of the party, I see through the open floor plan, is outside in the backyard that overlooks L.A.

The Baldwin Hills neighborhood and views have been one of the gems of Black L.A. for decades, but slowly and surely they are becoming less Black. Some of the party is downstairs in the kitchen, the guest quarters area, with marble countertops. It's a little dated, but fancy nonetheless. I find myself in the basement kitchen area making small talk with people, mostly those with red buttons. Not because I'm a home-wrecker but because I'm not trying to talk to

Green people because I'm not open to being rejected or rejecting people.

My phone rings and I step outside, away from much of the crowd, to answer. It's Harlem. He's in his first year of college, although he will take a semester off to refocus and take therapy seriously. He is enjoying life at a big university, and he feels the need to tell me about his partying. I am always available for my siblings when they call, especially Harlem. He's the baby and needs specific attention. I think losing parents so early in life carries deep effects. Lifelong.

"What's up, Har?" I answer, walking over to the edge of the heated pool, steam rising from the water.

"HEY, BIG BRO!" he yell/slurs.

He's been drinking, I can tell. I hate that he drinks. He's only eighteen. He knows I do not approve of him getting drunk, but I do not chastise him that much because I am fearful I'd have him feel as if he couldn't come to me for anything. So I'm mindful of how I talk to him while he's drunk.

"Harlem, sounds like you've had too much to drink. Where are you?"

"DOES IT?" he says, genuinely surprised. Still yelling. Still slurring.

"Yes."

"I've ONLY had two or three beers! I think, I think. Something called, like, like, API...no, no, IPAs!"

"Where are you?" I forcefully whisper, walking away from the pool and more toward the manicured desert garden, farther away from the party crowd. I can tell Harlem and I are about to have a longer conversation. I notice someone is trying to walk near me. This person will turn out to be Mario.

"I'm on campus. Where else would I be! I'm at a party. I stepped out to call you."

"Is that so. Is everything okay? I'm at a party, too."

"Really! You're at a party! Not Mr. Academic! What kind of party?"

"I actually have a life outside of school and you all." At that point, I actually did not. "I'm at a hook-up party."

"SHUT UP. YOU ARE NOT?!"

"You're right, I'm not." But I low-key am. I mean, a Red, Yellow, Green party? Go figure.

The guy who will turn out to be Mario, who I was gradually moving from for a private convo with my brother, stops inching toward me and is now sitting on a lounge chair by the pool and looking at the night sky. He thinks he's slick. I know when someone's checking me out.

"What's up, Harlem, what's on your mind?" I continue with my brother.

"This PARTttyyyy. Mostly everyone is…kinda…gayyy."

I know this fool didn't say what I think he said. *Gay* is not a negative epithet. Before I begin my mini-lecture about how using gay as a negative is less than intelligent—I try not to say things are stupid—as well as offensive, Harlem continues with his thought.

"I mean…Let me get my words together." He pauses and sounds like he's swallowing a wad of saliva. "Most of the people here are actually gay. Or bisexual. Pansexual. Yeah, pansexual, that's the word they are saying."

"Okay?" I say, confused to why he's calling me.

I'm at a party myself, surrounded by beautiful Brown-skinned cuties. He's at a queer party, okay, big deal, it's college. I almost slip and say *get your dick sucked and call me tomorrow*, because now I'm looking at ol' boy, who has been inching toward me. He's cute. And I know that if he's here at Jordan's party, he must have his shit together. Because Jordan's Black and bougie ass only keeps Black and bougie people in his circle.

"I've been drinking," Harlem says. "And now I'm thinking, Zai. How did you know you were…you know. Gay?"

"How did I know? Well, how did you know you were straight?"

There is a pause. These less-than-smart comments he makes, got to keep him thinking.

"Well, I don't know," Harlem says. "I mean…I *do* like girls.

But, I'm thinking, how do I know I *do not* like guys? I'm taking this sociology sexuality class and I got invited to this party by someone in the class. And now here I am three drinks in and…"

I'm too sober for this convo with Harlem. I look over at Mr. Inch-His-Way, wave my hand and make a gesture for me and him to have a drink. I know he has to understand my hand gesture asking for a drink. But he decides to pretend he doesn't understand and walks over to me.

"Hold on, Harlem," I say when Inch-His-Way approaches me. "What was that?"

"Hi, I'm Zaire," I say to Inch-His-Way, and hold the phone down to my chest so Harlem doesn't hear. "I'm on the phone with my little brother. He's at some party, questioning his sexuality, he's in college…Anywho, I'm trying to wrap up the conversation, but I need a drink to do it. I was hand gesturing asking if you could get me a drink, any drink. Do you drink?" I say this all too fast because I'm nervous, and Mr. Inch-His-Way is cute, and I'm sober, and that's what I do when I'm nervous, talk too damn fast, just like my sister Savannah.

"Zaire?" He smiles. "Mario."

"Yes."

"Nice to meet you, Zaire. I'll get you a drink. What would you actually like?"

"Thank you! You're saving me here," I say. "Since autumn is upon us, I'll have whiskey. Whiskey on ice or whiskey and a little ginger ale."

"I'll be back."

I watch him walk away. He has a very nice body and a sexy walk. A hint of a switch. I keep staring until I hear Harlem yelling through the phone.

"Helllooooo! You there, bro?"

"My bad, yes, I'm back."

"Okay, hurry, tell me," Harlem says. "How did you know?"

"I knew when I felt an attraction toward men," I say. "That's pretty much it. Then sexually, I had to experiment, see what I liked and didn't like."

"Bro, when you say it that way, it sounds simple."

That's because it is. Or it can be.

"Are you attracted to guys?" I ask, nervously. Do I really want to know this about my brother now?

"I mean, I do find some guys hot."

He didn't say attractive, he said hot. My goodness, another gay in the family. This news calls for a JamesGang family meeting, and I can't wait!

"I mean, I find girls hot, too," Harlem continues. "I've never had sex with a guy. I'm not going to lie, I've watched gay porn and bi porn. And I've gotten off to them both."

"Harlem, did I need to know that?"

"I think it's important information. Don't you?"

I see my drink coming toward me. Mario? Shit, I think that's his name. I know I need to get off this phone. I can't help my questioning little brother out right now, I'm supposed to be meeting people.

"Sure it is, Harlem," I say. "But listen, we can have this conversation tomorrow. You want to go to brunch?"

"Aww, man, I wanted you to tell me what I am," Harlem says. "But okay. Brunch tomorrow. Pick me up from campus, though, don't wanna lose my parking spot."

"Okay, I will," I say, and then back to older brother mode. "Be safe tonight. If you find someone attractive, then you find someone attractive, regardless of their gender. If you're out there having sex, use a condom! And if you're having anal sex, and you don't have a condom, use a lot of lube to reduce the tearing of skin! But definitely use a condom! Use silicone-based lube for condoms, it reduces the chance of tearing. Have fun and be safe. Harlem...don't forget. Use condoms!"

I'm rushing getting all of this out and talking too loud. I hang up. Mario? If that's his name, must think I'm a...he's back with my drink in hand.

"Here you go, Zaire," he says and hands me a red Solo cup. "Your whiskey ginger ale, courtesy of yours truly, the trusty bartender. *Salud!*"

I take a sip and it's 94 percent alcohol. Which is actually fine with me, I'm more of an on-ice kinda guy anyway. But I play coy. "My Lord, this is strong!"

"Stop it," he says. "You gave me the option of *on ice*, so don't play me. You like strong drinks."

"Ha ha, you caught me!" I say and laugh. "Thank you for the drink. Refresh my memory, what's your name again?"

"I'm Mario and you're welcome," he says. "Do you always order people to do things for you?"

"I do not. Not always. But I am the eldest of four."

"So…you do."

We laugh.

"I'm the baby of two," Mario says and gestures up the hill. "I live a couple houses up with my folks. I just moved back from DC this summer."

"Nice. Welcome back. What brings you back?"

"I graduated college and couldn't take another East Coast winter," he says. "So, I'm back, enjoyed a responsibility-free summer. Now I'm job searching and helping my mom out at the firm until I land a job."

"Must be nice." *Helping my mom out at the firm.* It really amazes me that there are people out there who do not truly have to stress about basic necessities like food and shelter because of parental support. "I'm in my last year of graduate school. Jordan and I go to school together."

"Yeah, I know. Jordan told me about you. He's my fraternity brother and childhood friend."

"When did he tell you about me?" I take a medium-size sip of my drink.

"When I was making you a drink."

I sip some more.

I wonder what Jordan said about me. Did he say I'm a nerd who doesn't have much of a life outside of school and looking after my siblings?

"But he didn't tell me you were a sexpert."

"A what?" I ask while taking another big gulp of my too strong, yet just right, drink.

"Sexpert," Mario says and lowers his eyes in a becoming come-hither look. "A sex expert. I overheard you telling your brother about condoms and lube."

I'm blushing inside. Hopefully, not outside. I may be a nerd, but I'm a cool sexpert nerd. But only those who have experienced my magic know this.

"I may know a thing or two about sex," I say, being a little cocky. Pun intended.

"Prove it, Mr. Green Button," Mario says.

We linger for a few seconds. I finish my drink.

"When, Sir Yellow Button?"

"My home is right over there." He points again to his parents' house up the hill. "The night is young and the yellow button is to keep people I don't want to talk to away."

"Nice," I say, referring to the house he's pointing to.

"It's nicer once you get inside."

I know Mario isn't talking about the house.

"I can imagine." I am not talking about the house.

"You don't have to," he says. "You can experience it. It's nice and clean too."

"Is that right?"

"When do you want to experience it, Z? Can I call you Z?"

"Sure. No one really calls me that. But it sounds nice with your tongue. And my drink is done. I'm waiting on you."

Mario chugs and finishes his drink.

"Everything is nicer with my tongue."

"Prove it," I say. It's definitely the whiskey making me say things like this to a stranger.

"Don't mind if I do. Let's go."

❖

That damn phone call from Mario. Got me going down memory lane. I'm not trying to go back.

Zaire

ICYF: Try Something New

Men are trash. Including me.

My sexy, almost-divorced ass is on the prowl. I've taken my siblings' advice and decided to waste time online instead of being in line at a bar or sitting here thinking about Mario. I've downloaded three apps in three days and I'm already kinda over it. You miss a lot being married, apparently.

My intention is to go on only when I have free time, but these little bastards are kind of addicting and they're annoying, too. I find myself going on during meetings, at the gym, driving in different neighborhoods, and when I'm about to sleep. I can't say I'm actually having a good time using them, but I can say the people I've engaged with are…entertaining.

Thanks to the apps I am partially questioning God or the universe as to why I am attracted to men. I have in my profile "not looking for sex." Which is basically truth. And yet all I get are ass and dick pics. Granted, Jack'd is mostly a sex app, but damn, sometimes, I just want to chat. Things can be so damn simple. Easy. Peaceful. But men make it so very hard. In the span of thirty-six hours, I've found myself chatting for five whole minutes, then realizing I'm over the conversation. And when I'm over it, I say *send me a pic* just to change the damn topic. And that's all it takes for two, three, or five pictures of every angle and every position to be sent. I find myself being the same person I do not like in others.

Trash. I'm basically the you're-cute-you-bore-me-send-me-body-pics-to-compensate-my-boredom type of online chatter. Just trash.

Since being single again, I have come to understand my attractiveness differently in these streets. I'm an inch over six feet tall, a whisper away from dark chocolate, a Black swimmer's body, which means, I'm slim, toned, but with a nice ass, and clean cut. I am learning in different ways, my physical appearance means different things for different ethnic communities.

On a Likert scale from one to ten, my ratings are as the following: Black areas, I'm a good 7.5 to 9. In Black & Brown areas, I'm a solid 7. In white places, like where I live now in WeHo, I'm anywhere between 4 and 7. In communities where they fetishize my Blackness, I'm a 10. I don't like fetishizers, nor being fetished.

I do not know how much longer I will be on these apps. I will report back to my rehab team, Savannah, Langston, and Harlem, letting them know I have tried. And trying is worth something, dammit, it's worth something. And I'm going to make me a cocktail for my efforts.

I will not post that. The rehab team is watching, after all.

KENNY

ICYF: You Never Know

The Inglewood Park Cemetery is beautiful as you drive into the front gates off Manchester Boulevard. In fact, the whole neighborhood is. It has changed majorly since the last time I was here. Nine years does a lot, apparently! Gentrification. The redevelopment of the Forum. The construction of a new football stadium. Vegan restaurants, coffee shop chains, and bike lanes. White women pushing baby jogging strollers. Stores just for pet food—not pets, pet food. Capitalism. Definitely not the same Inglewood I've been familiar with since moving to the West Coast. Everything just seems so pleasant now…and white-people, new-money, I-Wood beautiful.

Okay, so Carlos clocked me good by reminding me that I've never gone to see Jeremy Lopez, and that the last time was at his service nine years ago. I mean, we get busy. I got busy—responsibilities. But I'm here now. And truth be told, as scary as cemeteries can be—or at least are portrayed in most stories—there's something serene, tranquil, and beautiful about them. Sitting under the hot August sun, next to Jeremy's grave—not so beautiful. I don't like to be hot. But heat is a simple sacrifice to make, given that it's Jeremy's thirtieth birthday week, and I want to give myself and him the gift of closure.

When Jeremy died, I wrote a journal entry about the theme *beds*. Some being right, for the right occasion, and some being wrong. I wrote about newborns and their bassinets, pre-adolescents and their first bunk beds, college students and their first twin beds in the college dorm rooms, college graduates and their efficiency futons, and newlywed partners and their beds as a place of comfort, solace, and a place of life creation.

Beds.

Then I wrote about Jeremy and his beds. The bed in his bedroom at the back of his family's house that we used to sneak into for a quick moment of pleasure with each other. The hospital bed where he was given his last rites after being stabbed. The final bed, his resting place, where I am sitting now. For eternity.

It doesn't make sense that it took me nine years to get out here to see Jeremy Lopez. But it also does make sense. Jeremy and I were on and off most of our relationship. Just before his passing, I'd finally met and was accepted by his family. They said I was the one they counted on to help Jeremy grow up, get his life on track, be his fixer. At the time, also, I'd decided to give Jeremy one more try at making our mismatched-in-every-way relationship work. And then, like that, in hours, he was gone.

My thoughts come back to current day. I'm sitting on the dry green grass next to his grave site. I see his family has made the rounds for Jeremy's special day. Balloons, birthday cards, and family photos of all his brothers, his one sister, their kids, and their parents laid out across the gray flat stone depicting Jeremy's sunrise and sunset. I lay out one photo—the only one I saved from digital camera days—of Jeremy and me next to the other mementos. I pull out my phone to find Aretha Franklin's *Amazing Grace* album on one of the three music services I subscribe to. Aretha singing classic, old-school gospel—"You'll Never Walk Alone"—helps me get in a mood to do the homework my therapist Naija has encouraged me to do—write to Jeremy, read it out loud, release it, seek closure. The same, I'll do, eventually, with my mother. Also with Brandon-Malik, if I get that chance to have a face-to-face.

Once I've had my words with Jeremy—and I hope I'm not looking crazy to anyone watching me talk to a gravestone—I say a silent prayer, for myself and for Jeremy. Glad to get this one therapy homework assignment done. Glad that I didn't let it go to ten years since I've visited Jeremy.

I stand up, dust myself off, post a cemetery landscape shot to my IG storyline (just to see if Brandon-Malik notices, tries to contact me), and start to make my way down the lush grassy knoll. Careful not to disturb any of the adjacent grave sites and people sitting with their loved ones. As I get to my car, I hear a familiar sound—a group text notification from Carlos, Tyra, and Lily. I choose to not open it now, just wanting to be in my feelings for a moment.

"So you're just going to ignore your messages like that?"

I look up from my phone and am surprised to see him standing just a few feet from me.

"You?" I ask. "What are you doing here, of all places?"

Two hours later, I'm back at my condo in West Hollywood having drinks—yeah, more drinks, and dinner—yeah, more food—with Carlos. We've got Lily and Tyra on FaceTime on the living room big screen.

"So he asked you out in a cemetery?" Lily asks. Lake Merritt and parts of her Oakland neighborhood are behind her. She's a runner, like me, and taking a quick breather from her late afternoon laps around the lake.

"Talk about some stiff dick," Tyra chimes in from her Harlem, New York, apartment. It's nighttime over there and she's already told us she doesn't have a lot of FaceTime time—a first date with a new Tinder boo any minute now. "Y'all coulda been smashing all this time, Kenny, but you too slow."

"Give her your phone, Kenny," Lily says.

We all laugh at Tyra's signature line that usually moved us, even when we resisted, toward a romantic goal. Tyra was notorious for taking our phones and setting up post-class dates or hookups.

"I just wanna get to know Zaire, that's all," I say. I head into the living room from the kitchen, where I can view Tyra and Lily on the screen, and maybe catch a glimpse of Zaire returning home, but Carlos is sitting on the stool I like to sit on when I'm checking out what's happening in the neighborhood.

"Gotcha," Lily says.

"Besides, not a lot of Black people living in WeHo," I say. "And since we've been neighbors—he rents across the street—for a few months, I figured I could take him up on the offer for dinner together."

"Well, I applaud you, Kenny," Tyra says. "But I gotta go. My Lyft is downstairs."

"And I should get a few more miles in, guys," Lily adds. "See y'all soon, Docs!"

Carlos and I move back to the dining room after disconnecting FaceTime.

"The Inglewood cemetery, of all places?" His small plate of vegan pad thai is still full, but his wine glass is empty—as usual. "What a random place to meet your neighbor."

"Hey, what's that called? Coincidence? Serendipity?"

"Something like that," Carlos says and stands up. "I'm going to the bathroom."

I walk over to the front window again, look down and across the street. No sign of Zaire, or Zaire's car, yet. I guess he was telling the truth when he said he had a few family things to take care of today after the cemetery. Said he'd shoot me a text or get on FaceTime when he's back in the neighborhood. Not that I'm excited or giddy about meeting the guy across the street. I mean, he happens to look a lot like Brandon-Malik, but Zaire also seems like cool people. That part, I didn't tell Carlos, Lily, or Tyra, that when I see Zaire—especially—but one of his friends, too, I think of Brandon-Malik.

Truth is, I probably shouldn't be going out on dates with anyone right now. I'm a mess. Yeah, on the surface I've got a lot going for me. First, being that the odds have been stacked against me—all BlaQueer men, for that matter—since forever, well, it's noteworthy to have survived. I look good for a man pushing forty—good skin, good teeth, good thickness in all the right places. I run for fun and have good health—keep myself at the doctor and dentist regularly. I am a homeowner two times over. I have a doctorate degree. Got a few dollars in the bank thanks to good savings habits, home equity, and my mom's life insurance policy. I can be funny a few days a week and can also take care of business, get sophistirachet with the best of them when I want, and be thoughtful, considerate, and conscious. I'm #BlackExcellence, no ego. Just truth.

All that being said, though, how do you accept a date with someone new when your mind is still on the man who dumped you via text message? That's a question for Naija the therapist. That's a question I won't think about whenever Zaire decides to hit me up.

That truth, Zaire does not need to know.

ZAIRE

ICYF: The Dead Are Never Dead

I'm a mess. I remember reading in a book I don't remember, "But as bad as I am, I'm proud of the fact that I'm worse than I seem." And that's the truth. I don't know if you'd be proud of me here in the space I'm in, and that's why I had to come visit today. It's been too long anyway.

The day is perfect. The clouds are thick and the sun is blazing. It's the kind of heat that makes you sweat even if you're sitting pretty in the shade. I like this heat, reminds me of the South. Reminds me of the summer trips we'd take to visit your side of the family down in Lake Charles, Louisiana. It would be so hot and humid. Everyone complained except for you and me. The heat, the sweat never bothered us much. It's never this humid out here in Inglewood. I guess it's a sign I should be here. It's literally our kind of perfect weather.

All of the green hills are freshly cut. From where we are on top of the hill, we can see for what seems to be miles, rows and rows of freshly placed flowers. This particular spot is beautiful. The last time I came was right after Christmas, and the greenery wasn't so lush as it is now in the height of summer. I forget how gorgeous a resting place we chose.

I forget many things these days.

I'm sure you already know why I'm here. I need a moment to talk. I need a moment of clarity. I need to vent.

I need answers. I'm so damn needy these days—*pardon my language*—I do not know what to do. Get ready for the unload, Pop. You ready? Here goes...

Savannah is pregnant. Yup, you heard me right. Savannah Whitney James is about to be a mommy. She sent us a picture of the ultrasound. She and Anthony do not want to know the sex of the baby until they're here. Anthony even said the baby's gender isn't for the parents to decide. They're progressive this way. Savannah did a good job with Anthony. Although they hardly come around when we plan things as a little family. Regardless of that, quiet as it's kept, Savannah's actually the most put-together of the four of us, but I dare not publicly admit that to her stubborn ass. *Pardon my language.* Savannah also got us together to plan an intervention for me. Apparently I'm an alcoholic.

Langston is still, well, Langston. Nothing much to report here. The middlest of the children. Always in the middle of us, the peacemaker, the mediator. She's in cosmetology school. That biology degree didn't fill her up, so she's taking part-time classes for cosmetology. She should be complete with the program by next year. I'm still paying her phone bill and that expensive-ass credit card bill. I'm still paying a grown-ass person's bills that ain't my bills. Ain't that somethin?

Harlem is still dating. A lot. That boy sure do know how to love and lust a lot. He's on straight and queer online dating and sex apps. He's playing with all genders, sometimes at the same time and in the same damn room. He's also been the one to tell me about myself when I'm wildin out. He's kept many of my latest secrets from the other two JamesGang. One night I got so drunk at my favorite local bar, Trunks, that I called him crying about *God knows what*. Drunkish, I started to walk home from the bars and got as far as the CVS on La Cienega Blvd. But by the time I got there, Harlem had made it to me. He found me wandering and rambling aimlessly. Apparently, I was talking about you. About how I haven't spoken with you in so long and wished you were here to help me out, to help me figure how to get back to some sense of joy. You know when you left, my young brain told me to become the man of the house. That's such a horrible thing to think, to do, for a little Black boy, to have to think to become a man, whatever that is, especially as a kid. I've talked about you in therapy over the years. Then Mom died. Harlem said I should go back to therapy and start dating again. Dating away the pain is always Harlem's remedy for what ails.

I guess since I've already started talking about myself, I should *really* talk about my raggedy Black ass. *Pardon my language*. So much has happened since I was last here, Pop. I'm sorry I'm cursing so damn much, it's stress.

And I'm sorry I'm crying so much. I find myself crying on a damn dime. Watching a movie and some emotional-ass scene comes on. BOOM. Tears. I'm reading an article about a little girl who died in custody of ICE, then BOOM. Tears. The tears just overflow. It's a mess. And I'm so good at hiding these things. Most of my friends don't even know that although my divorce and my new life bring so many good things, the divorce and new life also bring these tears, and that I'm crying about things from past years. Last December I came here and told you something felt off with Mario and me, then a little over two months later, we separated and now we are full throttle on the divorce train. It was my call. I moved out a month after the separation. Then months later, I found myself in West Hollywood, where I never thought I'd end up.

A few months in with the divorce process and two online date fails later, here I am, Pop. Lying face down on the nicely manicured grass at your grave. My left hand pressed in the center of your headstone. I'm here for the first time this year. I appreciate you listening to my updates and all of what I'm carrying these past few weeks/months. Thanks for letting me lay here in silence for a few more minutes. I hope you hear that I feel deflated.

For years, since you've been gone and Mom's been gone, I've had so much of my life organized and put together for other people. I've had to have things together to take care of or support everyone else. My siblings, my close friends, and my mother after you died, rest her soul. Mom never truly recovered from losing you. She never really dated again, not seriously. I think she never allowed herself to truly be vulnerable with new people ever again. That denying herself a chance at love again, ate at her like a cancer, all the way until her broken heart ate her alive.

I feel myself starting another downward spiral because I've come to the thing. To the thing that is eating at me.

What if I never allow myself to truly open up again? What if I deny myself the possibility of wonder? What if love is just a theory? This is my fear.

"What do I do?"

If I wasn't rooted in Black Southern spirituality I would have possibly thought the heat was getting to me—perhaps I've been lying in the sun for far too long—because as sure as the sky is blue, I hear my dad talk to me.

Do what brings you joy.

I take my hand off the headstone, I get up because I know I'm not tripping. I am not scared. I remember all of the things I learned as a kid about how the dead are never dead. I remember Grandmama and Pawpaw telling stories and talking about how the dead will talk to you if you let them. I remember always hearing Mom in her room talking to Pops as if he never left.

So I ask back, "Is it really that simple?"

Do what makes you happy.

I get up from sitting. I throw my hands up to the sky.

"How do I do that?" I cry.

Keep trying.

❖

I'm walking down the hill, leaving Pops and holding on to his words, *keep trying.* It feels like that could be the answer, like my pops doesn't want any more sobbing from my crybaby ass. Feels like a demand. *Keep trying.*

Now I'm on the way to visit Mom. They are not resting near each other. Mom didn't want to be on a hill. She wrote in a letter directly to me before she went into the hospital for heart surgery that she wanted to be laid to rest under or close to a tree. The idea of being by shade and birds brought her comfort. So when she passed, we found the best tree available. It's about a seven-minute walk from Pop's resting place.

I begin my usual path when I'm here. Walk directly down the hill, past the building of niches of urns, past the garden of babies who've gone too early, and past the mausoleum. When I get to the pond, I take a moment to look at the water. Mom is resting about fifty feet away from the pond. I look around, and the day is still my kind of nice. From the distance I see someone walking. It's a familiar walk. Looks confident with a hint of timidness. That walk tells me that they are leaving from visiting someone they loved but they are quite ready to leave. This is probably a fresh loss. I begin to walk near them because even with the timid hue, that walk seems familiar. I've seen this person before.

When I get closer, I recognize him. The morning jogger. My neighbor. His walk tells me this visit was rough. He hasn't noticed me, and I think, maybe I'll brighten up his day. I use what I've heard Maya Angelou say, be a rainbow in someone else's cloud, to push me to say something to him.

KENNY

ICYF: They Haven't Stopped Living

The eleven o'clock news—with all the car chases, police shootings of unarmed Black people, frightened children and women all over the world, extreme weather everywhere, and angry men raising guns in the air—isn't how I planned to spend this weekend night. I thought I'd be with Zaire. Guess it's not meant to be.

I could call Mom to ask her what she cooking tomorrow, just for conversation, but it's too late on the East Coast.

Damn. I keep forgetting. Everything's too fresh.

I wonder if my sisters Tonya or Cecily do the same, start to call Mom and then remember...we can't. This reminds me of two things. One, I need to tell Naija the therapist more about my sisters, our upbringing, and how we've handled life since Mom died. It also reminds me I should probably call them, but their respective Ohio urban-suburban-living, raising-kids lifestyles means they're probably asleep now. Note to self: morning family FaceTime appointment. We promised we wouldn't go long times without being in touch, even with our cross-country lives.

I grab the remote, turn off the TV, and think about doing a midnight run through the neighborhood. But then I remember that it's late night, L.A., mostly white-ish neighborhood and that I could be mistaken for a criminal, so I nix that idea quick. Instead, I pull out the journal Naija the therapist says I should write in whenever I'm feeling some kinda way. And right now, I'm feeling some kinda way. My mom. Apparently ghosted by Zaire. And Brandon-Malik. Ugh.

I pick up the phone and go straight to Brandon-Malik's social media. I see the red circle, which means he's got a new storyline up since I last checked earlier today. He's also got a new pic up, posing shirtless with just bright orange swim briefs on a yellow lounge chair by a pool at a downtown L.A. hotel. He knows his angles, colors, skin tone, and lighting. Oh, how I miss those hands and that lean... Let me stop the fantasizing. I press the red circle to see his storyline. A BlaQueer pool party. Cute group shots of Black men of all shades and hues with their tight swim briefs. Someone new dancing up behind Brandon-Malik and about to plant a kiss on his neck. And then cut to the top floor and open patio of Fiesta Cantina in WeHo, and the same someone new with Brandon-Malik and they're boomeranging a quick peck on the lips. Ugh. He's living.

I toss the phone on the nightstand next to my bed and open the top drawer where I keep my journal. I start writing. No set topic. Random.

Why do I still want Brandon-Malik? What did we really have? What keeps me attracted? Why have I not responded to the "hi" text?

I'm attracted to someone who...is smart, Black, woke, tall...or at least taller than me, takes charge, makes decisions, is emotionally available and vulnerable, wants to raise woke kids, supports my crazy thoughts and wild dreams, lets me support his crazy thoughts and wild dreams, turns heads, turns heads but only has eyes for me, sees me as enough and doesn't have to seek what's lacking elsewhere, who can deal with someone who goes to therapy and is in his feelings and head quite a bit, who can nerd out with me on academics, pop culture, and Beyoncé, is Black-Black, has good politics, is pro-Black, and likes food...and the gym.

My ideal first date is...lots of fun, easy conversation, maybe some activity, and feels like no work. An ideal first date is something I've never had. I've always made the decisions. Paid for everything. Never really had first dates, just hangouts that turn into fucking that turn into regular and consistent fucking that turn into "we're hanging out."

Naija the therapist would say answer the question in the affirmative. Let me think on this more.

I miss my mom. I miss Brandon-Malik. I wonder what he's doing now at Fiesta. I wonder if he thinks of me. I wonder if he thinks of what we used to do together, how we'd spend time together. I wonder if it's all nothing to him. I wonder if all those "I love you" texts and words and DMs from him meant anything to him. I miss Brandon-Malik. Does he miss me?

I finish the entry on that blah note. I notice my phone has an unread text message, from a number I do not know.

Brunch @ 10am, my place? You know where I live. :)

Has Brandon-Malik gotten a new number, I wonder?

It's Zaire, btw.

❖

When I enter the propped-open front door, my first thought is that I'm in the wrong place...that I'm in *my* place. Zaire's rental apartment is the mirror image of the condo I'm purchasing across the street. Damn getting a mortgage when our places look the same.

"Zaire?"

I smell a mixture of breakfast in the air—definitely bacon, maybe potatoes, and most likely biscuits. The latest by H.E.R. is on, giving a nice and chill Sunday morning vibe. Someone's earning points for the food and music—#Effort. Someone'd earn more if the air was turned on. I guess he thinks propping a door helps. It doesn't.

"Kenny, you're early." Zaire peeks around the kitchen corner and smiles. He's wearing a Young, Gifted, and Black tank top, basketball shorts, and slides with black socks. Way more casual than the khaki shorts and black polo look I put effort into this morning. "You know gay *and* Black people never on time."

"You said ten." I look at my phone, wondering if I made a mistake or missed a spring forward or fall back. I definitely hadn't. "It's ten."

"You got jokes." He smiles, a hint of laughter.

"I'm punctual." I smile, make sure he sees me looking at my watch.

"Get a mimosa." Zaire points to a glass pitcher on the kitchen/bar counter, the front door closes behind me, and I help myself. "And then help me with the cheese, if you don't mind. I don't want to burn the eggs. I hate hard scrambled eggs."

I want to say I hate animal products for food, but since I'm not a life-or-death vegan, and Zaire *did* invite me over for brunch, I keep quiet. Naija the therapist would tell me to say something, I know, but I go, "Sounds good to me." I pour some mimosa and spot the block of cheddar sitting on a cutting board. Fresh cheese. #Points. "Thanks for the invite…neighbor."

"Cheers," Zaire says with a hint of a smile and a gaze that meets mine. A hint of curiosity. He also pulls out his phone. "To the BlaQueers of WeHo. I might tag you on my story," he says.

I notice he makes sure to only take a photo of our glasses clinking.

"Cheers," I say and sip and put the champagne flute down quickly. "It's burned."

"Is it? Lies…" Zaire sips again and I laugh. He's shook, looks confused.

"There was this show in the 90s—*Dynasty*." I go and take another full sip of the mimosa, just to reassure him it's good and I'm joking. "Diahann Carroll and some other diva reading each other over champagne and caviar…Someone sent me a clip this morning. I'll show you later."

"Oh. Ha. The cheese, please," Zaire says and takes the eggs

off the burner. "How old are you, Kenny? If you don't mind me asking."

"I'm thirty-nine. You?"

"I'm twenty-nine," he says while opening the oven. Definitely biscuits. I've got the grater and am making a pretty pile of cheese for two. "Not to sound cliché, but you don't look thirty-nine. Not that thirty-nine has a look. Well, maybe your Carlton-from-Fresh-Prince-outfit this morning does, but we clocked you for probably thirty-two…thirty-five at most. The boomerang turned out nice, did you check yet?"

"Checking now," I say, open my IG, add Zaire's story to my story, and wonder if there's a chance Brandon-Malik will watch and contact me. "Thanks."

The familiarity of this scene is comforting. Cooking together with a stranger, my neighbor. SZA now playing on Alexa. Zaire is confident making his way around the kitchen. The proximity helps me see Zaire has a good three inches in height over me.

"You caught that we think you look younger than thirty-nine," Zaire says. "When's your forty?"

"Next May," I say. "But I don't know if I wanna do anything. This past May was…"

"You don't have to explain," Zaire says. "We been checking you out. And if you do something, we want to be top of the list."

We laugh and clink glasses again.

"*We*?" I ask. "Have been checking *me* out? Explain, Zaire."

That's when I notice the dining room table has four place settings, a mixed bouquet of colorful flowers in the middle, and a BMW fob on the edge of the table, which looks out of place since I know neither Zaire nor his roommate drive a BMW. And Zaire's prepping an awful lot of food. This is not a brunch date for two. Ugh. What would Naija the therapist tell me to do?

"My roommate, Alberto," Zaire says and chuckles. "We call you Black Runner since you be up running all times of day and night."

If only Zaire knew what I call his roommate in my head, but instead I go, "You funny, Zaire."

"He may join us later." Zaire tops off our mimosas and tells Alexa to play Ella Mai. "He's in his room fucking—I cuss—no apology. Let's eat. Make your plate."

Definitely not a date, then, if Little Miss Hot Pants—what I call Zaire's roommate—is joining us. Ugh. I should've known better.

"For sure," I say. Despite a little disappointment that we may have guests on our date, I am appreciative for the company and the effort Zaire has put forth. "Thanks again for the invite."

The blackout day for my so-called vegan life is worth it. Zaire's cooking is amazing, flavorful, and full of fresh ingredients. He can't be a native of L.A.

"Where'd you say your people from again?" I ask Zaire, as he begins clearing away our empty plates—a sign of a succulent meal. We've already discussed everything from zodiac signs, the latest episode of *Insecure*, Black Lives Matter, white gentrification in South L.A., the influx of straight-owned and chain eateries and bars in WeHo, podcasts on our playlists, to what we're reading lately. We briefly talked exes, but wanting to stay in-the-moment, we agreed to leave the past in the past for the time being. He's legit, from what I can tell, and definitely woke—a plus on my list.

"Grew up in L.A., but my people from Louisiana," he says and pulls out another full pitcher from the refrigerator. "Want some?"

"Sure. Why not. Not driving and not working tomorrow."

"Lucky you," Zaire says. "A rich guy."

"Far from it," I say as Zaire places a full glass in front of me and sits next to me at the dining room table. I hate talking money, so I change back to the original question. "I grew up in Ohio, but my people from Tennessee on my dad's side, Alabama on my mom's side."

"What brought you to L.A.?" Zaire asks.

I'm liking the attention. Been a while since that getting-to-know-you energy came my way. Yep, Brandon-Malik. I also know this is the roundabout way of getting to the what-do-you-do question that we do in the BlaQueer community to size each other up. It's credential time. So I run through the roster of accomplishments.

"Moved here after finishing my master's. Worked at CUELA

for almost fifteen years doing diversity and social justice work outside of the classroom. Just quit after some life transitions and finishing my doctorate…"

"You're a doctor? Damn."

"Education," I say and continue. "Definitely not the same pay scale as medical doctors. Ha. So now I'm doing some consulting work mostly for higher ed campuses and organizations until I figure out my next chapter…like Oprah. Ha."

"What is your next chapter? Then I'll tell you mine."

"Do what Oprah does. Take the university to the streets. Put education into mass media. Help people who don't have the privilege to go to college to learn and to live their best lives. Definitely help people grow in their critical consciousness, speak truth to power, blah blah blah."

"That's dope, Kenny," Zaire says. I'm excited that he's attentive and paying attention. "I'm similar. That crazy. I worked at CUELA's rival, but recently took a job at a social media company doing the same kind of diversity work. I read, do research, do presentations. I might be interested in local politics— like putting some Black perspective into the WeHo City Council. Stuff like that. I'm a creative at heart, though, and might need some help figuring out my life. You down?"

"I'm down," I say. "Tell me one thing you've been reading lately?" I ask.

Then regret asking. Nerd alert. No one cares about reading in L.A.

"You for real?" Zaire asks. "Well, lately I been reading about charters vs public schools and Black communities."

"Ugh, charters," I interrupt. "Charters don't fit into social justice or with Black people, as far as I'm concerned. My opinion."

"But they do," Zaire interrupts. "We disagree, I see. But it's funny how our work is kinda similar."

"Definitely a coincidence."

"Anyway, L.A.'s home," Zaire says. "I'm figuring out life, too. Just moved into this place a couple months ago."

"Siblings? I'm the oldest of three. I've got two sisters, both are back in Ohio. One's an artist, one's a housewife. Our mom died in May. Remember, my complicated birthday?"

"Sorry to hear," Zaire says. "I'm the oldest of four—two sisters and a brother. We all have artsy names. God rest our parents' souls, I think they wanted to be artists."

"Loss is hard," I say. "But we keep their lives alive."

"One hundred," Zaire says and raises his glass. "I'll tell you more later, but back to this WeHo thang. How you like it here?"

"West Hollywood's weird, but it's home for me now, too."

"Same," Zaire says. "I'm still getting used to being in a mostly white neighborhood, though I appreciate the mostly queer part. It's convenient."

Convenient for what, I wonder. But say, "It has its pros and cons, but I could appreciate a few more Black folks around here. It's too damn expensive, though."

"Being Black in L.A. is weird," Zaire says. "And I grew up here."

"Being BlaQueer in L.A. is weird."

"Being Black-Black in L.A. is weird."

"But you're not a hotep Black, are you? They're weird."

"Definitely *not* a hotep," Zaire says. "We're not stuck in 1992. And yes, they are weird."

"Thank goodness, Zaire," I say. "I thought you were a hotep for a second, with that name. Is that your name-name or a chosen name?"

"It's my name-name," Zaire says and gives me an annoyed look. "Where'd you get a white-sounding 80s Black name like Kenny?"

"Truce. Okay. You're not weird."

"You're not weird."

"You're not weird."

"Black queer folks who live in West Hollywood don't even talk to each other. That's weird."

"But we're talking," I say and lean in and kiss Zaire. "Is this weird?"

Must be the sixth or seventh—I've lost count, by this time— mimosa giving me nerve and confidence. But surprisingly, Zaire leans in again and opens wide. And we're kissing again. And there's tongue. And I'm thinking of Brandon-Malik and I'm wondering: Is he kissing the guy I saw in his social media last night right now, if he kisses other guys on Sunday mornings, if he's been kissing other guys all summer, if he thinks of me, if he misses me like I miss him, if he's let himself go with other guys like I'm ready to let go with Zaire, my new neighbor whom I've barely met. I know Naija the therapist would tell me to be in the moment, so I put myself back in the moment kissing Zaire. Two Black men kissing in West Hollywood, something I've rarely seen or experienced. I hear this kind of interaction is more common in the valley or South L.A.

The experience is over.

Little Miss Hot Pants roommate and his plus-one emerge from a bedroom after a night of living his best life.

"Black Runner?" Little Miss Hot Pants squeals.

"Alberto!" Zaire backs away from me, stands up, adjusts the excitement in his basketball shorts, which is hard because I can tell he's not wearing underwear. I think he's embarrassed. I hope not.

"I know you, bih," Little Miss Hot Pants' companion says and points to me. He's got on his white shirt and black pants uniform from either last night's shift at Bossa Nova or preparing to go to work this morning.

"I know you know me, and I know you," I say. And then everything I've been attempting to work through, get over, live with this summer floods back to my mind because the guy in front of me is the one tangible connection to the one who dumped me. "You're Brandon-Malik's roommate!"

ZAIRE

ICYF: It Can Be Awkward

Alberto had a noisy night. Three rounds of fucking. I was high most of the evening, so it didn't bother me that much. If I'm honest, and I am because it's Sunday, the sounds turned me on. I find myself smoking and chilling at home on Saturday evenings since West Hollywood hip-hop nights where the Black people will be are mostly on Fridays and Sundays.

My family's advice is all over the place. Stop drinking. Get on apps. Date more. Whatever.

I've decided to take Harlem's advice and delete one of the three sex/social apps I've been on. The best part, however, is that I've been talking to two guys regularly for the past two weeks. One is from Jack'd and the other is from Tinder. They both are quite sexy.

Tinderoni's name is Joel, he's a twenty-seven-year-old Salvadoran nurse who lives in the valley and gives great head. I found that detail out a couple days ago during our first hangout.

Jack'd-boo's name is Elijah. He's intriguing, not only because his sex drive matches mine, apparently, but because the dude is a jack of all trades. We haven't met in person yet, but I like when we chat and FaceTime. He's twenty-eight, Black, makes most of his living as a math tutor in the Hills, but his passion is musical theater. He's a thespian.

Last night while high, I texted them both to see if either wanted to chill today—Sunday—but they both already had plans. My horny self felt attacked when they both couldn't hang out.

It was then that I remembered I never hit up my neighbor from across the street, Black Runner aka Kenny, so I sent him a text inviting him to brunch. It might be nice to get to know another Black West Hollywoodian.

❖

This morning, I have a clearer mind. I realize I texted Kenny in the wee hours of the night inviting him over to brunch. Texting a stranger during a time of the night when the only things open are legs can give a new date the wrong idea. He is sexy for someone who seems clean cut and polished, but I do not want him that way. And I do not want him to think I do. But I know, lately, I've been a little too friendly in my getting-a-divorce life. So, before I get out of my bed, I send a funny-serious text to Alberto:

> *Zaire has invited someone for brunch at 10am. He will make enough food for you and whoever that is in your room to have later. BUT Zaire needs help. If you notice you do not hear any noise in the living room, please come out. If there isn't any noise, that means Zaire is doing something his sober mind wouldn't want to do. Thanks for your support.—Zaire's Prevention Management*

I get out of the bed. When I head to the bathroom I shout to the living room, "Alexa, set Sunday mood!"

With that, the speakers in the living room and bathroom start to play Ariana Grande's "Thank U, Next."

After a couple of mimosas, I can totally see myself attempting to make babies whether it's with Kenny or someone else.

❖

I'm getting ready to preheat the oven for the biscuits when I hear a knock on the door. I look at the time on the microwave and it is exactly 10:00 a.m. Kenny is right on time. A punctual Black. He looks like the type.

"You're early," I say looking him up and down. He looks different from his jogs and from the time I saw him at the cemetery. He has a little scruff this morning, though, and is wearing khaki shorts and a black fitted polo. He's fit as fuck, I can tell up close and personal. And that scruff is cute. Maybe I should have rubbed one out in the shower after all. Damnit.

Kenny makes no fuss about me still preparing brunch. The only thing completely ready are the two alcoholic pitchers. One is a mimosa, typical champagne and orange juice; and the other is a vodmosa—a little surprise creation of vodka, sparkling cider, and lemonade. He joins in helping to prepare the food while we make small talk.

I find out he's grieving a loss, his mother. Although he doesn't say he's grieving, I know grief when I feel it, because I've been there. He's an academic, a doctor, Dr. Black Runner. He gives many compliments. He compliments the apartment and the socially conscious art. He compliments my cooking—notices all of the flavors, which makes me believe he must be a cook. He compliments my fade and my smile, which feels like flirting.

When we make it to the living room, I am buzzed and maybe we are sitting too close. Maybe we are staring too long into each other's eyes. Maybe I should renege on that text I sent to Alberto telling him to bring his ass out here if he doesn't hear any noise. Maybe…then Kenny kisses me. Then I kiss him. Then Alberto follows the fuck out of my text directions, and he and his Little Overnight Guy pop in like it's Christmas morning. Then, apparently Kenny and Little Overnight guy know each other.

Then Kenny gets up and excuses himself to the restroom. He looks shook and annoyed.

"How do you know Kenny, again?" I say, both puzzled and nosy.

"Oh, she dated, well fucked around with my roomie," Little Overnight Guy says while walking to the kitchen with Alberto. "A little over a year she was into my roomie."

"The food looks and smells delicious, Z!" Alberto dances in the kitchen. He's in an impeccable mood, and I'm glad he changes the subject. I don't want to know about Kenny's exes yet, and I'm not ready to talk about mine.

I do not hear the toilet flush or any water running, but I hear Kenny coming out of the bathroom.

"Hey, Zaire, thanks for brunch. I had a good time. I have to go."

Without looking at Alberto and Little Overnight Guy, he speed-walks out the front door.

From the large window facing Kenny's condo, I watch him walk-wobble across the street and into his complex.

That was awkward.

The kiss. The exit.

Just awkward.

KENNY

ICYF: Remember the Platinum Rule

So one thing you may not know is that I fall fast, but I'm not sure if I'm falling fast for Zaire. He's cool, cute, and all, and I really enjoyed the Sunday brunch hangout with him, until Little Miss Hot Pants and Brandon-Mulik's roommate interrupted us. Okay. Let me stop the misogynistic language and humanize them both with their real names—Alberto and Preston.

I'm not gonna lie. The energy was off from the beginning. I mean, who picks up in a cemetery? And who says yes to being picked up in a cemetery? And who accepts that a midnight text is an acceptable way to initiate and accept a date? Yeah, I know I've been out of the dating circuit for a while and this is how things are done these days—I'm not that old. And who goes on a date when they're in mourning over the loss of a parent and mourning the loss of a romantic relationship? I'm so fucked up. I'm a mess. I know I need to stop saying that, because I'm really not a fucked-up mess. I'm just... in transition.

Zaire. Yeah. The energy got weirder when Alberto and Preston appeared and lingered. It's almost as if they were trying to get rid of me. So I got rid of myself and left.

Stumbled drunk across the street to my condo and passed out on the living room sofa, and barely got up in time to semi-enjoy Insecure.

I haven't returned any of Zaire's texts, nor have I responded to the notes he's left on my car. Now I'm ghosting. And I'm sure he sees my every move, given that we stay across the street from each other. I've been doing like we used to do when the Jehovah's Witnesses would be coming down the street when I was a kid—lay low, out of sight of the front window, keep the blinds closed, sound low, and don't answer the door. Yeah, he's been by a few times. I got notes on my door, too, and I know he's worried about me.

What's weirded me out more is not hearing from Brandon-Malik. Especially after running into Preston, his roommate, the way we did. You'd think Preston would be like, "Bih, when's the last time you talked to Kenny, because I just saw that bih at my dick appointment's place, and he looking good and getting back out there in these streets, so you better get back with him before you lose him to my dick appointment's roommate."

But that didn't happen. Isn't happening. And it's probably a sign that Brandon-Malik is definitely in the past and that I should move on.

And still...I'm a piece of shit and fucked up because I'm more fixated on being dumped by Brandon-Malik than I am with the fact that my mom has died, and that my sisters have their respective spouses and children to help them mourn, and that I'm alone in L.A., a place where no one really knows or cares about me, and that the only person I can confide these things in...is you. Because therapy is a privilege and a choice. And I pay you.

❖

Luckily, Naija doesn't take offense to my snide remark about paying her to listen to me and she offers me a piece of homework. The Platinum Rule. Treat others the way they would want to be treated. Don't ghost the way I perceived I've been ghosted. So, here goes making amends…

❖

Since I don't work regularly, and Zaire does, I figured I could cook a meal for Zaire to enjoy after his eight-plus hours at the dot-com. I'm putting the finishing touches on what I hope will be a delicious dinner —braised chicken thighs rubbed in Cajun spices (yeah, no vegan today), red beans and rice, a simple tossed salad with tomatoes and cucumbers, and for dessert, banana pudding (definitely, no vegan!)—that will make up for the delicious Sunday brunch Zaire cooked a couple weekends earlier. But this time, the only drinks are water or juice. I don't want a replay of the embarrassment of a few weeks ago.

The buzzer rings, indicating that Zaire is at my gate, and I ask Alexa to put on *The Read* podcast, something to keep the mood both woke and comedic, just in case Zaire and I can't figure out conversation.

"Hey," I say as I open the front door. I'm hesitant and he appears the same. He looks tired but handsome in a fitted red polo, pink ankle pants, and stylish gray sneakers. I forgot how casual-chic is the new professional look in most fields now outside of higher education. Not that I'm missing my 9-to-5 at the university. Fuck that.

"Hey."

"Come on…" He makes his way in without asking and takes a seat at the bar that separates the kitchen from the dining room/living room space. He sets his leather work bag on the empty stool next to where he's sitting. "In."

"Hi, Kenny."

"Zaire," I say. "Sooooo, I cooked. How was work?"

"I can smell," Zaire says. "Work was fine. Nothing major."

"Cool."

"You? Do anything toward your university-for-the-masses dream today?"

"Nothing major."

"Get on it," Zaire says. "Time waits for no one."

The small talk is small…and gawky.

"Aaaand this is awkward," I say and offer Zaire a cold bottled water from the refrigerator. "Truce. I apologize. Only water today. Not doing too much like last time."

Zaire stares and laughs.

"You're weird, Kenny."

"You're weird, Zaire."

"*You're* weird."

"*You're* weird."

We start a stare-off competition. Until Zaire breaks the hold.

"If I'm so weird, Kenny, why you trying to make up with me by cooking me dinner?"

I don't know what to say, other than the truth right now. "I'm sorry. There."

"Define…sorry," Zaire says half serious, half joking. "Apology accepted. There."

"It was just awkward, you know," I say. "Seeing Preston there with your roommate. I used to date Preston's roommate. And it was just weird. I haven't been with anyone since my ex this spring."

I should tell Zaire that I think I'm still dating Brandon-Malik, as far as I'm concerned, because I haven't responded to his *hi* text, and that Brandon-Malik is just taking a break until he can come back to me, ready to be 100 percent for me. But I don't.

"Well, we haven't been with each other yet," Zaire says and looks in my eyes. "Unless you're telling me that's whassup."

"All water under the bridge," I say, changing the subject. I've probably already said too much, giving Zaire Brandon-Malik's name, the connection to Preston, all that. I'm sure he knew all this anyway. "Besides, L.A.—well, BlaQueer L.A.—is too small for us not to all be connected or know someone we've dated or slept with. I'm over it."

Lies. I'm not. But who needs to know that but me right now.

"I'm not trying to get caught up in some drama with exes, roommates, roommates' exes, all that," Zaire says. "I'm trying to get caught up in you. And this dinner."

"Oh yeah, dinner. I hope you don't mind," I say as I'm assuming he's going to want as much as I'm heaping upon his plate. "Figured you'd be hungry. And since we're not drinking tonight…"

"Nah, I hope you don't mind," he says and pulls out a marijuana vape pen. I do mind, but I don't get to say it quick enough. Takes one hit until the buzzer vibrates. "I'm appreciating your company again, Kenny. Glad we can make amends."

Zaire follows me just across the way to the dining room, where I've set our plates down.

"Same here."

"Come here, weirdo," Zaire says and pulls me into his arms and a kiss. "Don't fuck up again like that, and definitely don't go ghost on me."

"Promise."

"'Cause if we're going to have a little neighbors with benefits situation going…"

"Who said we're benefitting? Yet?" I give him a short peck and lead him the short way to the dining room table to eat. "Alexa, play Ari Lennox."

"Alexa, play The Carters Essentials," Zaire says, overshadowing my request.

"You're so difficult, Zaire."

"You're funny," Zaire says, takes the chair next to me, and pulls out his phone. Shows me the screen. Two tickets for Beyoncé and Jay-Z the following week. "Wanna go with?"

"We haven't even gotten through dinner, let alone this little hangout…date…whatever you call it," I say, knowing full well I want to go see the Queen and King, because when the tickets went on sale I was in the midst of funeral planning and just forgot to buy tickets. "You gotta be someone special to offer a floor seat to someone you've just met."

"I got a feeling about you," Zaire says. "You down or not?"

"I'm down," I say. And although I've told myself not to think about Brandon-Malik, he pops into my head. Wondering what he's doing tonight. If he's going out on dates. If he's fucking anyone else. If he's thinking about sucking someone off tonight, the way I'm thinking I'm gonna do Zaire before this dinner-date-reconciliation-redemption-tour thing ends. If only Zaire could read my mind. My entire mind. "Thanks for the invite."

"Thanks for saying yes," Zaire says and begins eating. "And damn, thanks for dinner. This is legit."

More dinner conversation. Feels a lot less pressured than the first time. Thanks to no alcohol, though Zaire's taken a couple more hits off his pen. I wonder how he'll wake up on time in the morning. Whenever I have done pot, it's made me sleep so hard that I've been unable to function the day after…and the day after that. Zaire must be a pro. No judgment.

"I hope you enjoyed…and enjoy," I say, as I bring our post-dinner sweets to the table. Bowls of banana pudding.

"You've just made this Louisiana descendent happy," Zaire says. "And banana pudding is my absolute fucking favorite. I might have to wife you the fuck up."

"Just wanna make you happy," I say and let my eyes linger a little longer than normal conversation. Just to send a message. "If you wanna be happy."

"I'm happy, Kenny," Zaire says and in like three spoonsful, it seems, his banana pudding is gone. Like that.

I savor a couple bites of dessert, when I hear my phone chime. It's a text from Carlos.

"I gotta get this," I say and head to the bar, where my phone sits. "My bestie and his boo are having a Labor Day weekend gathering— it's a couple days after Beyoncé. He needs my confirmation and guests. Sorry."

Zaire follows me into the kitchen, spoons me from behind, while also checking the phone as I reply. Ha. Doesn't believe me? Jealous?

"Tell him yes," Zaire says and kisses the back of my neck.

"And tell him you're bringing me…and my roomie and his date… if it's not too much."

Presumptuous, I think.

And I should probably mention the gathering is in Palm Springs. Presumptuous. Happens, when there's no real communication taking place. At least I'm honest about where my, our, skills lack right now.

But I text Carlos a quick reply. *Yes, plus three. Send deets later.*

Zaire presses up behind me, again, while planting tiny kisses on my neck, ears. Puts my phone on the counter and turns me to face him.

"Now," he says, moves my hands down below his belt line, and stares into my eyes. I'm in the moment, but I'm also in a Brandon-Malik moment, remembering *our* first time taking it there. A similar approach and scene. Like they're kindred spirits or something. Damn. Zaire squeezes his hand over mine as I slowly undo the zipper of his pink work pants. "I think Zaire's ready for happy. You?"

ZAIRE

ICYF: Stop the Reindeer Games

"Wait. So why did you invite him to the Beyoncé concert?"

Jada, my favorite coworker, is yelling through my car speaker. It's our little ritual to call each other on the morning commute. Makes the traffic bearable.

"Because I'm a mess!" I yell through my car Bluetooth. Late. Per. Usual. On my way to work.

"Well, you and I both know that," Jada tells me. She's already at work. Early. Typical. Virgo. "But give me more."

"I was in the heat of the moment," I say. "He made me dinner and the food was bomb AF." I pause. "And then he apologized for ghosting—you remember that Sunday brunch drama? So, I thought *why not?*"

"But you know *why not?*"

"Do IIIII?" I sing.

"Hell yes!" Jada says. "You don't even like him like *that!*"

"I knowwww! But I was feeling good with a full belly and did I mention I was high?" I'm trying to get her to support my bad decision. She will not budge.

"And what?"

"Jada, I felt bad. He just lost his mama! Bless her soul. And he's actually a good catch. On paper he's amazing!"

"Don't bring his mama into this, rest her soul," Jada says.

"Oop."

"But you are correct. On paper. Zaire, on paper he's amazing," she says and pauses. "Do you live on paper?"

"Well, technically no."

"Technically, metaphorically…it's a no all the way around."

She is right. I have no business taking Kenny to the concert. I do not like him like *that*. He likes me. I *think*. I'm wise enough to know that I shouldn't lie to myself for too long. So I admit to myself that I usually think about Kenny when I'm horny or bored. This is an irrefutable truth that I cannot express verbally this morning.

❖

It has been four years since the last On the Run concert. My siblings and Mario—the ex I'm still not divorced from—sat in the best seats $200 tickets could afford then. We got to the concert early, pregamed, and I do not know what possessed me, then, to take some gummy edibles from the person standing in front of us. But I did. The entire day leading up to the concert, Mario had been worried about our attire, saying we *had* to coordinate. That was stressful. We had plenty of clothes in our closets but Mario insisted we get new clothes for Queen Bey and Hov. We looked good. We got many compliments both in person at the concert and on Mario's social media accounts. Yay. Four years ago. Mario and I were young and full of possibilities. Life seemed a bit more possible. We sang and cried all night. At one point it started to rain and the crowd got more hyped. There we all were—Savannah, Langston, Harlem, Mario, and me, at the end of summer, jumping up and down, singing "Young Forever," being young, Black, and free. We were all high, drunk, or both. Everything slow motion. Everything good for the moment.

This time around at the concert, things felt different. Bey and Jay outdid themselves as usual, as expected. I am unsure how they do it, especially Beyoncé, but she is magic. She's amazing at every performance, and just when you think she can't improve, what does she do—improve.

I wish my love life and savings account had that kind of sauce. For this concert I had floor seats, a major improvement from four years earlier, thanks to my job. Working at a top tier social media company has its perks. In exchange, all I had to do was record a few VIP concert goers, asking them to make up a hashtag to describe their concert experience. I got that done before the concert began so that I could give my 100 percent to Kenny.

Kenny was cool with it all.

He looked cute. I could tell he really tried to look summer chic, with what appeared to be a completely new outfit from either Zara or Topman, just slightly more expensive and sophisticated than Forever 21 and H&M where most of the younger concert goers shopped. He wore a flowy floral print button-down shirt, painted-on jean shorts that emphasized his fit legs and ass, and white Nike classics with black crew-length socks. I wore my favorite weekend shirt, my vintage green Ninja Turtle T-shirt, jean shorts, and a thin jean jacket with two medium-size jacket pins, one reading "I Still Believe Anita Hill" and the other reading "Fuck Fronteras" that I got from an event put on by the artist Chucha. We looked cute together and got compliments, just like Mario and I did four years earlier.

We danced the whole night. Kenny felt like a best fr…, associate, colleague, something like a good acquaintance. It started off feeling like an intimate romantic date. Which didn't sit that well with me. But there I was experiencing two of the greatest entertainers of our time, floor seats, potentially leading a good person on, being irresponsible and playing reindeer games. The guilt became the third wheel on the date. That is when I brought out my special pen. I took three puffs. I looked over at Kenny knowing he usually doesn't partake, but tonight was special, or at least I made it appear like it was. I look him in the eyes and told him to let his wig down and be *forever young.*

❖

"Hello! Zaire, you still there!" Jada whisper yells through my car speakers to get my attention.

"Yes! I zoned out thinking about the concert."

So much so, that now, I'm turning into our parking structure.

"I think you're leading him on, Zaire."

"I'm not."

I can't find parking. Every day that ends in a "y" is the worst when it comes to finding parking at work. Well, finding parking that I like. I could easily park on the top uncovered floor where no one wants to park, but that's too far from my office, so I continue to circle around the first three floors.

"Did y'all kiss?"

She's so damn nosy. We did kiss. It was euphoric being in the presence of Black magic masked as Beyoncé and Jay-Z. Of course I kissed him. He's a good catch—on paper. We kissed during the finale, "Apeshit." There may have been some oral satisfaction, too, in my car as we waited for the parking lot line to die down to leave the venue. #TintedWindows. It took over an hour to exit anyway.

I get annoyed, give in, and drive to the tenth and uncovered floor. I need to get to work and see Jada's facial expressions as I tell her more about Kenny.

"One innocent little kiss," I say. Half truth.

"Seeeeee, games. Reindeer games."

I finally park.

"Ugh. Why am I this way?"

"Because you do not know how to hoe right, Zaire," Jada says. "I've tried to tell you, do not get attached to people you aren't seriously interested in. Your divorce is almost final. You NEED to hoe around. Do not boo-up your fucks."

"I am hoeing wrong huh?" I ask. Then it dawns on me. "Oh shit, Labor Day is this weekend."

"Hell yeah," Jada says. "Gonna be a slow, lazy week. Thank God."

"I promised Kenny I'd go to Palm Springs with him this weekend," I say. "Shit. I can't cancel. Not after Beyoncé…Hashtag Hoeing All Wrong."

"All wrong, niece." Jada laughs. "Reindeer games."

"Tragic."

"Indeed," she says. "But hurry up and get in here, I have to tell you about Lamar's latest shituation."

I sit in the car for another three minutes thinking about OTR 1 and OTR 2. How different I was during each concert. How the feeling of freeness felt different. Kenny enjoyed himself, or at least it appeared like he did. I hope I did a good job at masking my conflictedness in regard to us. He's a good person. He's smart, funny, and sexy. He just isn't for me, and I do not understand why.

Before I get out of the car, I tell myself I cannot tell Jada I also saw Mario at the concert. He was seated just three rows ahead of Kenny and me. He made it a point to lock eyes with me twice. The first was during "Me, Myself & I," the other was during *our* song. The song that made us feel most young and most free together—"Young Forever."

KENNY

ICYF: We Can Be Messy

It's Labor Day weekend. Yay! I've decided to take Naija the therapist's homework with me. And so here I am, waiting out in front of my condo with four bags—mine, Zaire's, Alberto's, and Preston's. I'm creating family in L.A. My fourth hangout with Zaire in a couple weeks. So unexpected. We're off to Carlos and Ricky's new place in Palm Springs. This is going to be interesting. At least I hope it is.

❖

Carlos and Ricky have thought of everything.

The perfect hosts, they instructed us to bring nothing but ourselves and our bags. And I can see why.

There are swimsuits in every size in the outdoor cabana. The two refrigerators are fully stocked with food and snacks in one and beer, wine, and mixers in the other. The bar is glistening with more Ciroc, Bacardi, Henny, White Henny, Hendricks, and Jack than we could possibly consume this long weekend.

They've even got a cook to meal prep for us and a housekeeper to clean up.

And it's a good thing Ricky and his gay hospital work crew are here, just in case—the public bathroom everyone can use off the main living room is stocked with all the medicinals, prescriptions, edibles, and poppables we want, no questions asked.

How Carlos with his university student life job and Ricky with his EMT life job are affording all this, I don't know, but I am curious.

All I know is that the dozen or so of us Carlos and Ricky invited to Palm Springs are going to have a great weekend. And that's without Beyoncé being a headliner in the nearby vicinity. I really need this, I think. Naija the therapist thinks so, too.

Carlos assigned Zaire, Alberto, Preston, and me to a sizeable suite near the back of the house, adjacent to where Carlos and Ricky will be sleeping. We've got a sliding door to the deck and the pool. #Goals. We've also got two queen-size beds, so decisions have to be made.

"So, who's sleeping where?" I ask.

It's awkward, but not really. As far as I know, Alberto and Preston don't know I gave up the goods to Zaire against my kitchen wall, nor after OTR 2, but then again, I don't know Zaire's ability to hold secrets or not. Not that we're a secret. We're not anything. We're just all so connected, and I don't want Preston saying anything to Brandon-Malik about me possibly dating Zaire— though we're *not* dating—just in case Brandon-Malik decides to come to his senses and get back with me. One can hope none of this has happened.

"Bih, please," Preston says and jumps in the bed on the left side of the room, closest to the bathroom. He shoos his hands toward the bed on the right side of the room. I never knew he was this funny, all this time I was dating his roommate, Brandon-Malik. Cute, too. That racially ambiguous kind of light-skinned Black guy that the world—especially the West Hollywood world—loves. "You and Zaire over there."

"Case closed," Alberto says, jumps next to Preston, and spoons him. "No peeking and no crossing over in the middle of the night."

"Never been an issue," Zaire says. "Ain't gonna be now, heffa."

Zaire grabs my bag and his and moves them both toward the closet and dressers on our side of the room. Alberto and Preston, I can hear, are exchanging saliva and moans. Already. Damn.

Zaire turns to me and whispers, "Thanks for inviting me...

us. We cool, right? This?" And points to the bed. "'Cause if this makes you feel weird—you, me. I'm cool sleeping on the deck. I'm a nature boy."

Zaire pulls his marijuana pen out his bag—for emphasis of his nature boy nature.

"No issue here," I go.

"Cool," Zaire says. "That's whassup. Wanna take a hit?"

"We just got here," I say. "No judgment."

"Judgment. I feel attacked."

"I just wanna take in everything," I say. "This big house, the guys, the desert, the heat...being out here with you. Not that we have any labels or rules or anything."

"We don't," Zaire says. Bluntly. And it's truth I don't want to hear. Much like Brandon-Malik made clear early on in our hanging-out life. "No rules, no labels, no commitments."

But you took me to OTR 2. You came out to Palm Springs with me—invited yourself, your roommate, and your roommate's Grindr boo, I want to say. If that's not something, when you could have done a million other things over Labor Day weekend, then what is it?

But instead, I counter, awkwardly, with, "You're weird."

"No, you're weird," Zaire says. "Inviting strangers to your best friends' new place in Palm Springs. It's called 'boundaries.'"

I'm shook. And don't know what exactly to say. Again. I want to speak louder than the whispering we've been doing only out of respect for Alberto and Preston—who are definitely into each other. They could go rub one out in the adjacent bathroom, if they need it that bad, right now.

"Then why'd you come out to Palm Springs with me if I'm so weird, Zaire?"

"'Cause you're weird, Kenny."

"So why are we here, then?" I ask. I'm insulted and feeling stupid for bringing Zaire, Alberto, and Preston here, if this is what the weekend will be like. "Because you can Lyft back to L.A. if you want."

We stare. An impasse. I'm really confused. And kinda getting turned on hearing Alberto and Preston doing their thing on the bed ten feet away from us. I think about the parking lot session after the Beyoncé concert, too. That was hot. But I'm more than a kitchen wall, steamy-windows-in-a-car kinda guy. Much. More. I just need to voice it.

"I'm just playing with you, bro," Zaire says. Smiles. Offers up a fist bump. Then a hug.

"Is this how you joke?" I ask. "'Cause you're weird. I don't like that."

"It's 'cause you're weird, Kenny," Zaire says. "And I like weird. You're cool people."

"I thought you were cool people," I say. "But now…"

"Kiss me," he says, grabs my hand like he did in my kitchen last time we shared a meal together, and helps me start to undo his zipper. "Zaire's ready for happy."

I'm resistant and hold my hand still. So many thoughts, but I don't know if I'm ready for that kind of happy with Zaire now, less than an hour into our Palm Springs weekend. I haven't even properly introduced Carlos and Ricky to Zaire, Alberto, and Preston. And *we're* in *their* home as guests. And Zaire wants to whip it out with Alberto and Preston just feet away from us? Ugh. I wish Brandon-Malik was here, instead. Ugh.

"Okay, sorry," Zaire says. "I think we need a drink. Or a hit of something."

Zaire motions his vape pen my way. I nod no and he takes a hit.

"I'm cool," I say. "We're cool. You're right. We need some food, drink, pharmaceuticals, and we'll be cool."

"Gimme a kiss and we'll be cool right now."

He smiles. I smile back. Naija the therapist would probably say something about red flags, but I'm not giving a fuck about what Naija the therapist says now. I wanna be in the now. And not think about anything. But I do.

I'm not drunk, yet, but definitely attracted. So I will not lean in for a kiss, yet, though I want to.

I give Zaire a kiss. Ugh.

"That's my Kenny," he says. "Take care of *this* now."

I motion over to Alberto and Preston, who are hot and heavy, and probably wouldn't mind Zaire and me getting hot and heavy. But I resist and take my hand off Zaire's zipper.

I'm confused.

I will not ask Zaire what our against-the-kitchen-wall session meant at my place, though I want to. I will not ask what the kiss during "Apeshit" meant, or the head action in the parking lot post-concert meant, though I want to. Or what his joking/arguing approach is all about, though I want to. Or if he is serious about us not being anything to each other...the no rules, no labels, no commitments thing he said.

I will not think about Brandon-Malik—rather, I will *try* not to think about Brandon-Malik, though I want to. I miss Brandon-Malik.

I will not ask Preston *anything* about Brandon-Malik this weekend—not that he's untangling from Alberto any time soon—though I want to.

I'm like the cool queer kids say—I'm not here for a long time, but I'm here—in Palm Springs, with Zaire, Alberto, and Preston—for a good time. And I want to medicate myself. Stop the thinking. I mean, we are in Palm Springs, after all.

"Hoes, can y'all shut the fuck up, please? Or kiss, fuck, or whatever?" Preston yells across the room. I thought Zaire and I were whispering and that Alberto and Preston were gearing up for round one. "'Cause y'all weird."

❖

Day two. Shades are down, but the sounds of loud house music wakes me up. I hear splashing in the pool outside our bedroom window and the aroma of barbecue seeping through the vents. I tap my watch and it's almost noon. Damn. I never sleep this late. I think I must have had too much to drink and not enough food. Lucky, no hangover. I reach over to cuddle Zaire, but the bed is empty. Roll over to look at Alberto's and Preston's side of the room.

"Hey, did y'all hear Zaire get up?"

"No, bih, did you hear Alberto get up?" Preston is perched on his side and staring at me. "I think they wanted to hike or something before sunrise."

"It's afternoon now," I say. "Zaire never told me anything about wanting to hike…though he is a nature boy, if you know what I mean."

"He gets high, bih." Preston gets up from under the covers and sits on the side of his bed. He's naked and sits there like nothing, skinny and tight six-pack with a nice happy trail leading down from his navel to his…it's larger than life and it's soft. Hate that I looked. "It's Palm Springs, bih. Clothing optional. Don't be a prude."

"I'm not," I say. "I just don't know you like that."

"If it makes you more comfortable, bih, I'll put on some clothes," he says, grabs a pair of boxer briefs, and puts on a yellow Bey-chella (BAK) tank top. I guess that's who Brandon-Malik took to Coachella with our tickets, when I was dissertating. Just before everything began to end. Just weeks before the *I can't be there for you* text. At least it was Preston, and not some other date. A real date. "I'm hungry. And I stink. Smell like I just got freshly fucked. Which I did, bih. Did you?"

We share a quick laugh. I roll out of bed and sit on the side.

"Nah, Zaire and I…we're not like that," I lie. Just in case he's reporting back anything to Brandon-Malik. "Just friends. No labels, no rules…"

"No titles, no commitments," Preston says. "Sounds like the book of Brandon-Malik rubbed off on you."

That's my in. Maybe. I don't want to use Preston, though, but I would like to know something. Preston is my only lifeline and connection to Brandon-Malik.

"I guess," I say. "Yeah, I guess."

"Um, so what's up with you and Zaire, really?" Preston asks. "'Cause you're a nice person, and I've always thought it, and I'm just kinda getting to know Alberto and Zaire, you know. So what's up?"

"Well…" I will not say anything about feelings, though he's gotta know that Zaire and I have hung out on numerous occasions.

The Brandon-Malik factor keeps me from being authentic and being friendly with Preston. "Well, we aren't anything specific."

"No labels, no rules, no titles, no commitments," he says. "Yep, you and Brandon-Malik are the same. So damned noncommittal about your feelings."

I want to go, "Brandon-Malik's got feelings?" But instead, say, "I barely knew you when I was hanging out with Brandon-Malik. What are you saying?"

He walks over and sits next to me on my bed.

"I'm his roommate," he starts. "Now I'm not giving away company secrets or anything like that, 'cause he's my boy. But all I'll say is he knew...and I saw...what a great catch you are, Kenny."

"That's nice of you to say." I fist-bump Preston. "Thanks, friend."

"I'ma start calling you 'Zaddy, Daddy, Doctor Graddy,'" Preston says, laughs, and gives me a hug. I admire his loyalty to Brandon-Malik. He's cool people. "I can't believe our dates left us alone like this."

"Woulda been nice for Zaire and Alberto to say something."

"Dumb heauxs."

"We should shower and eat something," I say. "I'll introduce you to Carlos and Ricky and the guys, so you have some people to hang out with. Sure you don't wanna be stuck with me waiting on our guys to come back."

"Tiny violins, Zaddy Daddy," Preston says, rubbing his fingers together. "I don't mind being alone with you." There's that tiny violin again. In a millisecond I think about my mom, how she's really dead. No one tells you that any and everything can remind you about those you've lost. I bring myself to this moment.

"I don't mind being alone with you, either," I say. "You're funnier than I got to know from when Brandon-Malik and I were hanging out."

Our eyes kinda linger, but then I look at my watch to stop the moment.

"Well, as I recall, you were either rushing in straight to Brandon-Malik's room, so we never talked," Preston says. "Or you and he were heading out to some big event. Always a big event, you and him. And yeah, bih, I'm wearing Beychella gear. Thanks for sharing your tickets with a nigga. I love Beyoncé, too."

"Glad you enjoyed it, Preston," I say. "My dissertation season was too much for me to go. Glad it was you and not some other…"

"Brandon-Malik had someone lined up," Preston says. "But I told him that woulda been a major fail and foul, and that you'd never forgive him for that. Glad he listened."

"Thanks for looking out for my feelings, Preston."

"You're good people, Kenny," Preston goes. "Even someone like me—just out for a good time—can see that."

We laugh and fist-bump and linger eyes and talk some more and before we know it, it's almost four and we haven't left the room, showered, eaten, drank, or reunited with Alberto and Zaire. Where are they? Still no word, though Preston and I have left a few texts with our respective dates.

"Okay," Preston says. "You shower first. I'll grab food and some cocktails. Then I'll shower, and we'll chill for a bit. Maybe you should text again?"

An hour later, we've both showered, changed into clean clothes, gotten a quick *I'm ok and back soon* text from Zaire, and heard many of the houseguests leaving to head into the gayborhood of Palm Springs, where apparently Alberto and Zaire have been all day after their hike.

"Dumb asses," Preston says, carrying a bottle of Honey Jack in one hand and handing me a drink he's mixed up in the other. "They'll have their fun and we'll have ours. Cheers!"

We're sitting on the back patio by the pool. The sun is starting to set, a reminder that Zaire and Alberto have been gone all day. If Zaire's losing interest he could say something. He doesn't have to lie.

"Cheers," I say with little enthusiasm. I'm feeling a bit deflated with this Zaire disappearing act. I sip. "Damn, Preston, this is good."

"It's those restaurant and bar skills, Zaddy Daddy," he says and clinks glasses with mine. "See, if you actually had talked to me

IN CASE YOU FORGOT

whenever you and Brandon-Malik were creeping into the apartment, you woulda gotten a taste of my skills. Oh well."

I look at my watch, to distract myself from wanting to ask about Brandon-Malik. I feel good that I haven't looked at any of Brandon-Malik's social media since spending the day with Preston.

"We should eat something," I say. "You hungry?"

"Bih, try this." Preston opens a plastic bag with a brownie in it. "Just a tiny bite. Chill with me."

I'm not a prude like Preston thinks I am, so I take a little more than a tiny bite. "See? I'm a pro."

"If you say so, Zaddy Daddy." He sips from the Honey Jack bottle. "What's up?"

"Nothing," I say. Though I wanna say I'm confused about Zaire, confused about Brandon-Malik. Thoughts are everywhere. "Just chillin out here with you. While our dates are living it up at the bars in Palm Springs."

"Is he really your date, Kenny, if he accepted your invite out here, and he's spent the day elsewhere?"

"I don't know."

"You've got a lot more...what's the word? Resiliency than I would have," Preston says. "Dumped by my roommate, though I think he misses you. And don't repeat this or get your hopes up, because once Brandon-Malik's done, he's done. Fragile masculinity, all that academic shit y'all doctors talk."

"He does? Miss me?"

"All I'm going to say is he knows he fucked up," Preston says. "He mentions you from time to time. I know all about your community university idea for dumb, basic heauxs like me. He really put you up on a pedestal. Like no one I've known him to fuck around with."

Well, damn. The answer to the $64,000-dollar question. I think.

"And here's another thing, Zaddy Daddy." Preston takes another sip out the bottle and I can tell he's feeling the high take effect. I know, because he's a good thirty pounds lighter than me and I feel it coming on quick. "Zaire ain't shit. At least from what I can tell from the nights I crash with Alberto at their place."

"Really?"

"I mean, when you said y'all noncommittal and shit," Preston says, "it's because he can't commit. He's still trying to get divorced from his husband."

Zaire's married? I think I'm shook. So I go, "Zaire's married?"

"Bih, I'm high. Don't say I said anything."

Zaire's married? "Fuck."

"You're a good man, Zaddy," Preston says and sips from the bottle again. "Don't say anything. Kiss me."

I'm flattered but, despite the brownie definitely taking effect, I go, "You're cute, Preston, but I can't. You and Alberto. Me, Zaire. Brandon-Malik."

"Feel this," Preston sets his bottle down and puts a hand on each of my forearms. Runs the fingers up and down my arms.

It's magical. I close my eyes. I'm floating. Definitely not here, but yet, still here, in the moment in the Palm Springs heat.

"Oh my God."

"You like?"

"Yeah," I say and open my eyes. "I can't."

I stare into Preston's eyes. He stares back. I'm trying not to think about Zaire. Or that Preston is Brandon-Malik's roommate. Or that I feel so fucking good right now.

"Alberto and me are open."

"You're right."

"Zaire is married."

"Right again."

"You can."

And I do.

ZAIRE

ICYF: Fuck'em

Kenny and Preston fucked.

Alberto fucked Carlos.

Then Ricky fucked Alberto.

I got the fuck out of there.

Took a Lyft back to L.A., like Kenny suggested I do in the first place. I used Kenny's credit card to pay for it.

FALL

KENNY

ICYF: Get Back Up

So I guess you could say I really fucked things up. So much so that Zaire refuses to take my calls, texts, or DMs. Alberto gives me the stank-eye when we pass each other on the street while I'm running or he's coming up the street from Santa Monica Boulevard with his grocery bags in hand. Preston has gone ghost, no surprise there, not that we have any way to contact each other other than through Bossa Nova. And absolutely no word from Brandon-Malik. Still.

I've been blocked. From everyone, it seems. Can't see Preston's social media, everything's on private. Can't find Zaire's social media anywhere, though I used to be able to find him easily. Brandon-Malik's posting the same-old same-old—gym selfies, abs pics, biceps curls pics, #TBTs to summer days by the pool at that DTLA hotel he frequented in the summer, storylines seeking clients for whatever fitness, consulting, modeling, stylist, OnlyFans business he says he's operating these days to make whatever living he wants the world to think he's making.

Tell you this. I'm never touching edibles again. I acted a fucking fool in Palm Springs and I'm 100 percent embarrassed about the weekend.

What do you mean that I will need to find a new therapist? I like coming here and talking to you. Yeah, I know I'm not the best with my homework and following up on what we discuss, but I promise I'll be a better client.

Oh, it's not that?

Then what is it?

Conflict of interest? How?

Oh my. I'm sorry to hear about your mother.

At least you've got a few weeks, not that it's any consolation. I wish I'd had time to prepare. Look at me, fucking it up again and not thinking and making it about me. I'm sorry for what you're going through. Thanks for your time and for listening to me these past weeks. I know I'm a mess, and hopefully the new person taking your patients will be just as good as you. But I wish you the best, Naija.

❖

Hi, Thea, I'm Kenny. I'm a mess. But I don't want to be a mess.

Naija the therapist said you don't play, and that's why she referred me to you and your private practice, and I'm really ready to make therapy work this time. I have a lot to unload and work through. But first, you don't know anyone named Brandon-Malik or Preston, do you? Or still fixated on an ex who ghosted you via text? Or have any family in Ohio? Or lost your mom recently? Or just earned a doctorate degree, quit your job like you've got Oprah money, and trying to figure out life? Or sold your house in the suburbs and downgraded to a small condo in West Hollywood?

No? Just trying to get all the conflicts of interest out of the way first.

Okay. We're good then. I'm ready to do the work. I'm ready to get back up.

Wait, you mean right now? We're starting right now? I haven't even told you everything on my mind. Oh, that's right. Naija the therapist gave you my file.

All right. I'm ready. What are we doing? I mean, what am I doing?

ZAIRE

ICYF: The Hoetation Has Its Flaws

Back on the apps after the Kenny and Palm Springs mess.

But sometimes you get tired of the hookups. Sometimes the rotation—*hoetation* is not enough.

Don't get me wrong, ever since I re-introduced myself as a single dude to the app hookup world, I've had a pretty good hoetation. I have an after SundayFunday bae. I have a Tuesday night situation. And I have a whenever-I-feel-like-something contact named Max, he's always down. Plus, Kenny was a brief thing, though I didn't meet him on the apps.

Getting my bearings was difficult at first. I got online and overthought everything and questioned my sauce. Some app tells you how close the person is to you, others inform you about who's seen your profile, and others you have to match to chat.

So I found myself questioning, *Do I hit him up first? What do I say? Do I have to type in complete sentences? Is a simple "hi" enough? How many questions do we need to ask before we inevitably meet to "hang out"? Are emojis too immature? Do I send nudes or do I unlock my private pictures?*

I quickly found my groove. I can tell after three texts back and forth what the situation is going to be.

In the beginning, my profile picture was a full body picture of me outside of my apartment next to a palm tree. My *about me* section was a paragraph, written in complete sentences. Looked something like this. "Hi, I'm newly single. I'm not here seeking sex. Open to good vibes and good chill people. New to the area and would like to meet friends. If you'd like to know more, I'm down to share. Hit me up."

This time around, my profile reads, "Hit me up. Hung and plumped, if it goes there."

What a difference a day makes. Or, rather, a few weeks.

❖

I'm getting home from having an excellent fuck with Max. Three blocks away, it's a quick walk home. The October night, cool and quiet. Alberto is boo'd up in his room. It's the second week of autumn, definitely cuffing season, and I guess Preston will be Alberto's seasonal boo for sure, even after the Palm Springs shituation. Yay.

I go to the bathroom and turn on the shower. I set the water temperature a little hotter than usual; I'd like the bathroom to fog up before I get in.

Max was good. But I think this is my last time hooking up with him. I think I'm over this.

If I'm not drinking, I'm fucking.

If I'm not fucking, I'm at the gym.

If I'm not at the gym, I'm reading some article for work.

This is my life. It's not bad, it's just not where I thought I'd be on the cusp of thirty.

Tonight, I would like to be boo'd up. I'd like to have someone special to make autumn wondrous.

Instead, my night was like this:

At 8:30 p.m., I sent Max a text of an eggplant emoji.

He replied within forty-five seconds with a peach emoji and asked what time.

I told him now.

He said give him thirty minutes to clean.

And shortly after nine I was at his door.

He greeted me with a crop top and jock strap. I enjoyed our hour together of passionate sex.

But now it's 10:30 p.m. and I'm back in my apartment looking at myself in the bathroom mirror, waiting for it to fog up so I can let the water from the shower be the warm and intimate hug I desperately need tonight.

Shower done.

I stand dripping wet in the foggy mirror. I use my left hand to wipe enough to see most of my reflection. This is a very melodramatic moment. Maybe I'm making it dramatic. Kiana Ledé's "One of Them Days" is playing and the song resonates with me tonight.

I admire my nice forming chest. I notice my abs are starting to bulk up and have some definition. Post-separation-almost-divorced-body is in full effect, and I'm not mad at my reflection.

I brush my teeth with this new charcoal toothpaste. My teeth are black. I start to smile with black teeth and this makes me laugh. Who in the hell is using charcoal toothpaste? I am, trying to get my nearly perfect teeth to be more perfect, more white, because living in WeHo has really started to affect my sense of personal beauty. I have to keep up with these WeHo heauxs. Walking down Santa Monica Blvd., everyone is gym body perfect. Then you walk down Melrose Blvd., and everyone looks as if they are all starring in the same young trendy/hip-hop music video.

I live dap in the middle of this.

So here I am trying to have my teeth as white as snow, using the latest dental (or is it?) trend—charcoal. A mess.

I pick up my phone to take a picture of my black mouth to send to my siblings. They will have a laugh at my expense.

And like that, I decide to delete Tinder. I figure deleting these apps one by one may help in centering myself again.

Somehow.

❖

I'm five days in without sex. With someone else. I've jacked off every day, sometimes twice or thrice in a day. I do not know what it is, but I'm less than two months shy of thirty and my sex drive is high. I told myself I wasn't going to hook up with anyone random anymore. I'm putting an end to the hoetation. For now. I want to give myself a chance again. To meet someone. I think I'm ready to really be out there and to allow myself to be uninterested in some people.

I've allowed the fear of me not being interested in people hold me up from trying to make a connection.

As soon as I get to work, I decide to ask the math tutor/musical theater thespian, Elijah, out on a proper date. We've chatted every day for the past couple weeks. Nothing major. Just talk. But good talk. I go on Jack'd, go to his name, and message, *Morning thespian. Would you like to go on a date this Saturday? If you're busy that's okay. Here's my number anyway, 310-555-5555.* Elijah reads it within minutes.

An hour, no reply. I get the clue that I probably misread our daily talking.

I'm set to delete the app. I check one last time during my lunch, and he replies, *I've been waiting for you to ask. I have a play to attend Saturday night, but I'm open Saturday morning and afternoon.* :)

I am clueless how to respond because I'm overjoyed with this date. I overthink. After five minutes, I reply with, *Bet.*

Bet, as in I'm trying not to sound overly excited. Bet, as in I'm cool. Bet, as in I'm freaking out. Bet, as in I almost became depressed at the idea that he didn't want to go on a date. Bet, as in I haven't been really excited about a date in so very long. Bet, as in what in the hell are we going to do this Saturday afternoon?

After I reply, I run to Jada for daytime date ideas. While on my search for Jada I get a phone notification from Kenny. I roll my eyes.

KENNY

ICYF: Do the Homework

The first thing Thea the therapist does is put me on what she calls "an entire breakup treatment plan." Because, as she says, I can't move forward with mourning and healing every other transition in my life that I've told her about until I deal with Brandon-Malik, Zaire, and Preston. All of them—the men in my life—she deems the low-hanging fruit in my therapy process. That she said, "them niggas ain't shit to your healing or your glory as Kenny Kane," and then asked for me to pardon her French because she called Brandon-Malik, Zaire, and Preston "niggas" in a therapy session— well, that sealed the deal for me that I would be sticking with her.

Reminds me of my mom. Which is why I like Thea the therapist.

She's quite different than Naija the therapist, who I loved, with her sisterly, let's sit and get centered, peace and blessings approach with me. Thea the therapist is like an older aunt but is only in her thirties, who tells me like it is, misses no beats, picks up on any and all inconsistencies, and infuses, sparingly, bits of her life experiences that relate to what I'm sharing. What Thea the therapist does, like Naija the therapist did, is introduce some African spiritual practices into the approach to healing. I'm at peace, feeling confident, and completely comfortable in Thea the therapist's care.

But this "entire breakup treatment plan." I don't know.

Looks quite simple, on paper, though I wonder if, in practice, I'm going to be able to do it and make it habit for the next thirty days to start with, ninety days a goal.

1.　Stay off their social media. Their, meaning Brandon-Malik's, Zaire's, and Preston's. No scrolling, no checking to see who likes any of their posts, no clicking on profiles of their followers or new people they've started following, no watching their stories of what they're doing daily, no adding the people who are frequent likers of their pages and posts, no checking to see what posts or pics they like or comment on, etc...Thea the therapist would like me to stay off all social media for thirty days, if possible. That part—all social media—I've got to think about.

2.　Reflection and journal writing about whatever is on my mind—that does not involve Brandon-Malik, Preston, and Zaire. Thea the therapist would like me to start writing about what I was feeling around my doctoral and birthday time, when Mom, Cecily, Tonya, and all our family from Ohio, plus my L.A. friends and classmates, were together in the springtime. She asks that I frame the thoughts in joy. Only in joy—what I was feeling, and what I saw and felt from the family and friends around me. I'm ashamed that my thoughts drift to Brandon-Malik, and I mention that Brandon-Malik was an integral support part of my final dissertation writing days, came to my graduation, and met my family. As an auntie would, Thea the therapist stares at me, says, "The Instagram model who ended things via text message...and, well, where is he now?" and continues with the plan.

3.　Re-center and shift any thoughts that come up of Brandon-Malik, Zaire, and Preston. Basically, as soon as they come up—especially the "I wonder where," "I wonder if," "I wonder what" thoughts, because we're human and they *will* come—acknowledge that I'm having them, but then quickly shift my thinking to something else. Keeping the journal handy, Thea the therapist says, in order to note when, how, and the frequency of the thoughts will help me. As Thea the therapist says, "Believe me, he ain't wondering where, if, or what about you. If he was, you know where he'd be."

4. Stay away from Brandon-Malik, Zaire, and Preston. This includes avoiding going anywhere that I know I'll have a high probability of running into any of them. Which is like everywhere, duh. But nah, I know that if I wanted to see any of them, I could do it. But I won't. Includes staring out my upstairs front window to stare across the street into Zaire's window. Includes Friday nights at Trunks, where Brandon-Malik loves to congregate with all his other IG-popular friends. Includes deliberately going running through the neighborhood at times when I know Zaire, Alberto, and Preston are leaving for the day or coming home from their respective jobs. I try to tell Thea the therapist that West Hollywood is small—barely two square miles—and that I can't *not* live, that I can't *not* leave the house, and she goes, "Kenny, you're smart. You *know* that you know how to run into people—you're not doing that!"

5. Detox and decolonize my diet. In other words, get back to vegan eating. Reduce or eliminate sugar, processed foods, and anything not from the ground. Water. Vitamins. Smoothies made from scratch. From there, keep running, add meditation, hire a trainer to come by a few times a week to train me in the gym at the condo's fitness center—shouldn't be hard, seems everyone is a trainer in this part of L.A. anyway. I'm definitely not doing the natural deodorant, soap, toothpaste thing, though. I'm not going "patchouli."

6. Focus on goals other than men. "You're a doctor fucking around in a sea of barnacles and leeches," Thea the therapist says, and reminds me of the visions for my life that I shared with her—university in the community,

helping people live their best lives, and commitment to a socially just world. "You're magic, Kenny, and I want you to see that. I mean, there's a reason why spirit led you to see CUELA wasn't for you anymore. Stay still and listen to spirit."

This, in itself, is worth the few dollars I'm paying out-of-pocket for today's session. Of course, less if I still had insurance through CUELA, but not going there now.

"Think you can agree to these?" Thea the therapist asks, and offers me her hands. "Let's give it thirty days, though ninety days is optimal. That'll get us to and through the winter holidays. And we'll do next steps with your grief after that. Sooner, if you feel ready."

"Ninety days. All this?" I look at the list of the "entire breakup plan" and feel overwhelmed, but then it pops in my head that I completed a doctoral degree and a dissertation this year, all while working a full-time job. I'm kinda resilient, definitely capable, and in most circles the shit.

"We'll check in every week to track your progress, or less, depending on what works for you."

"I will do my best."

"I think you can," she says. "I *know* you can. *You* know you can."

"I've got no other choice. I've got to get back to the me I've forgotten."

"You've got to discover the you you've never truly known before."

"You've confused me with that one, Thea."

"You'll understand when you understand," she says. "Now, excuse yourself out. Our time here today is whole."

ZAIRE

ICYF: Little Things Are Big

Elijah sent me an address and asked me to meet him at 11:30 a.m.

It happens to be two miles away from where I live, so I decide to walk. On good days, like today when it's not too hot or too cold for fall, I enjoy walking. I've become more comfortable with enjoying the outside, noticing and finding new things about the place I've called home for nearly half a year. The other day I stumbled upon a Black-owned barbershop off LaBrea. Now I do not have to visit the southside for my weekly fade.

I'm a few minutes early and I think he may have given me the wrong address because the navigation has taken me to an empty building across from a park. Nerves start to settle in because I'm anxious to finally meet Elijah. This date is the only thing I have scheduled to do this Saturday. I hope we are able to hold a conversation and have a good time at least for an hour. I'm not the best at in-person conversation with strangers, although it appears I'm an expert at it, especially because I've been known to be a sly flirt. Only a few people actually know the preparation it takes ahead of time for me to craft conversations and comebacks. I've never been on a first date that I didn't plan. I haven't been on a first date since Mario, to be honest, and Kenny and the app hookups—I'm not counting. This shit is new and makes me too damn nervous. Do I like this? I mean, *will* I like this, is the question.

"Is it hung and plumped?" a voice says from behind my left shoulder.

I turn around and it's Elijah in the flesh, live in color. It's a bonus he looks even better in person than he does on FaceTime. He's wearing a simple black T-shirt with "RESIST" written in white font, a fanny pack across his chest, gray jeans, and what used to be *white* Chuck Taylor shoes, now a smog gray color. I love his in-person look and style. Despite his nice clothes, the best part of his outfit is his smile. Those teeth and full lips. My God.

"Good one," I say and laugh. "Good morning, Elijah, nice to meet you IRL!"

He smiles and leans in for a hug.

"You haven't answered my question," he says in my ear.

This excites me, and I feel a thump in my pants.

"One thing about me that you may come to find out, Elijah, is I do not lie...often."

We release each other from a hug that's gone a few seconds too long.

Elijah stares me up and down. He's checking me out from the front. Hopefully he doesn't notice I have a chubby. He smirks when his eyes meet my zipper. Damn, he notices. If my nose wasn't the only thing that could get red easily, he'd notice I'm blushing.

"Time may tell if that is true or not," Elijah says. "Here, I come bearing gifts. Some breakfast."

Elijah hands me a KIND blueberry breakfast bar and a reused jam jar with some green juice inside it.

I want to say, "It's almost noon, I ate breakfast a while ago. I'm damn near hungry for lunch. I actually thought we'd be meeting at a place to eat and talk. You know, a typical first date." But instead I say, "Thanks. What's in the jar and where are we?"

"Oh!" Elijah says in a high pitch; he's excited for some reason. "I thought I told you what I have for breakfast most days. In case you forgot, the juice is actually kombucha with a little kale and ginger. I like to be active, so the juice helps in keeping my energy and health up."

"That's right. You did tell me. I didn't forget," I say.

I do remember chatting early on during our Jack'd phase about some of our personal daily routines. I told him some of my routines include stretching every morning and talking to plants in the morning. He told me about kombucha. I do not tell him I still do not know what kombucha really is. I will drink it and find out.

"Good," he says. "Don't forget the little things. Those are what really matter."

He has a familiar sparkle in his eyes. I already know I can stare into those warm brown eyes for hours and still find beauty. I need to watch myself.

"To answer your second question," Elijah continues, "we are at my favorite underground pop-up thrift store—PopShop. We have to hurry and go to the back because it looks like no one is waiting around outside so we can go inside now!"

Elijah grabs my hand and pulls me to the back of the building. No one is outside. It's a warehouse with a freshly painted green door.

From the outside, the building appears empty as fuck, but when you enter it is quite active. It's like Goodwill and Melrose Blvd. joined forces and birthed PopShop.

Elijah gives me the rundown of the this wardrobe cult. You follow them online to be one of their over 500k followers. Put your notifications on. Four days before they pop up in either New York, Los Angeles, DC, Miami, or Barstow, CA—apparently one of the creators of PopShop is from Barstow and people make a weekend trip out to the desert location—they start to post clues about where they'll be for the weekend. Then the day before the pop-up, they post a picture of the street sign intersection, and then it's the followers' job to find the warehouse/building with a freshly painted green door. Once you're there you cannot linger around or make a line outside the door. You're only allowed beyond the inside line if you follow PopShop social media.

"I've never been to anything like this," I say, looking around at all the local trendsetters and modern art.

"I'm glad your first time is with me. Let's try to get Halloween things! Do you like Halloween?"

Elijah is walking down an aisle of clothes touching most things he passes. My stomach is responding to the kombucha.

"Yeah, I like Halloween," I say. "It's cool. I guess I'll celebrate this year because I live in West Hollywood now. It's practically a city holiday."

"I love Halloween! It should be a national holiday. It's the one time in the year where many people dare to allow their imagination to run wild." Elijah stops walking and turns to face me. "People lessen their rigid ideas of body, of gender, of expression. I wish we could be like that always."

My stomach feels like someone is jumping inside it, not in a painful way, but in a I-may-have-to-go-to-the-restroom kind of way, and Elijah can notice something is off.

"You okay?"

"I think so," I say, scanning the venue for a restroom. "My stomach feels kind of weird."

"Yeahhhh. It's the kombucha. It's cleaning your insides. You probably have to have a bowel movement. The restroom is over there. I'll walk you."

Elijah points his finger to the corner of the room. I laugh at his bluntness and his choice of words.

"What's funny, Zaire?"

"I guess you are. For starters, it's our first date and you tell me I have to shit and you use *bowel movement*. Who uses that?" I laugh.

"Well, do you not have to…*shit*?"

"I suppose I do."

"Well, then," he pauses and continues, "this whole first date thing, it's so overrated. We are meeting in real life for the first time, but we've talked for weeks online already. Which, by the way, I honestly thought we were going to be online associates, because we hadn't met yet and we talked often enough."

We make it to the restroom, finally, and I whisper to myself, "Whew, child, the ghetto."

"I know you're fully human so you have other bodily functions besides cumming, Mr. Hung and Plumped."

He laughs.

"Touché, cutie. Are you going to come inside the restroom with me and smell my aroma since we're already so close?"

"Nope, I'll pass for now. I'll wait for you out here."

PopShop is low-key fancy. The decorations in the restroom are nice as hell. And to top it off, the toilet paper isn't that thin-ass paper shit you get in most public places. PopShop said if our cult is willing to find us with three clues and pay $25 for a pair of socks, we will give them high-quality toilet paper. Come'on Quill! The little things.

❖

PopShop is a cute experience. The only thing we buy are graphic socks. Elijah notices them in a bin and throws me a black pair with red roses. Says I look like the rose type—thorny and beautiful. He chooses a gray pair with a dolphin on each sock. I remember he said once dolphins are one of his favorites. I do not know why I remember this random fact about Elijah.

After about an hour of PopShop browsing, we're both open to eat—food. Real food. Elijah suggests we go to Smorgsasburg in DTLA, where we'd be able to eat from a variety of food trucks, have adult drinks if we want, and continue browsing for clothes if we choose. I'm having such a good time just being with Elijah it doesn't matter what we do. We call a Lyft and split the cost to downtown.

The ride is musical. Mohammad, our driver, gives us full radio control. Elijah says the game we are playing is Carpool Karaoke. We have to sing the song the other person chooses, and it doesn't matter if we don't know the choice, we have to make up something.

"Bet," I tell him.

Although we are technically eight miles away from our next location, downtown L.A., traffic guarantees us a good twenty-five or more minutes of songs. I play Beyoncé's "Signs" first. A quarter into the song, Elijah is doing so well, hitting every note, every word, I have to change it. I tell him I'm able to make up a rule because it's almost my birthday. I make him smile with that one. I find myself attempting to make him smile and laugh often. He has the best grin.

Next, I play the Roots' "You Got Me." He doesn't know all of the words, but he slays most of it. I'm shook. This Black-ecoconsious-fashionista-mathematician-actor is vibing out to a classic by the Roots?

Mohammad the driver is jammin out, too.

"You know Jilly from Philly was the original singer?" Mohammad fades in as the song fades out. "I'm from Philly."

"I didn't know that," I say. "That's dope!"

"I sure did know that." Elijah smiles and looks me in the eyes.

On Elijah's turn, he's determined to make sure I struggle. He asks Mohammed to choose the decade. I do not know what in the hell possesses Mohammed to choose the 70s. As Elijah scans the TIDAL selection of 70s music, he remembers I mentioned my birthday is coming—the week after Halloween, November fourth.

"Scorpio," he says and looks up from the phone and into my face with a smirk.

"Correct, and it's true what they say," I reply, not really knowing what people say about Scorpios besides they like sex. But, if that's all that's said about us, then that's fine.

We laugh. He says I must sing for my life because this is one of his favorite songs to karaoke. When he presses play, I immediately know it.

Who knew the ninth-grade choir selection of Queen's "Bohemian Rhapsody" would pay off and make me cool in the back seat of a Lyft one day?

Elijah joins in singing he's just a poor boy and stops singing, then continues at all the backgrounds. We eventually sing the song together. Full out belting. I sound terrible, but that isn't the point. I know that isn't the point because I stop singing once and say I sound awful. Elijah tells me it's not about how we sound *singing* together, he says the magic is in the *creating* and *being* together; being young, Black, and free in all the ways that we can. Not only is he talented and gorgeous, this guy is…brilliant.

So much for being uninterested.

❖

Earlier, this morning, when Alberto and I rotated our tandem parked cars, I knew I would possibly be gone for most of the day. I wanted to share with him that I was nervous about this date. But, because he and I aren't really talking like that anymore, since Palm Springs—I'm still in my feels about his current boo Preston fucking Kenny, I just said, "Wish me luck," to which he replied, "Luck! But, for what?" and I walked off.

Had I told him I was finally meeting up with someone I've been talking to for a few weeks, he would have told me to go with the vibe. So because I didn't actually have the conversation with him, I've been holding on to my own advice that I'm sure Alberto would have told me, too—just go with it. And going with it is what I've done all day. That's how I've ended up here at the Ace Hotel with Elijah.

It's a great date. Things happen.

I mean, we were having such a good time at PopShop, then at the food trucks, that neither one of us wanted to end our first date. We ate tacos and had a couple drinks. When the time came for him to head to Ace Hotel to help set up for his production, he asked if I wanted to join.

"You have plans after this?" he asked.

For a second I thought about lying and saying I did, just to seem as if I was busy. You know, L.A. sometimes makes me feel like I have to be, or appear to be, booked and busy all the time to impress people. Everyone's favorite response is *let me check my calendar*, or *let me get back to you*, or my personal favorite, *I think I have something, I'll hit you*. Rarely is it an automatic definite—*Yes, I'm free*.

"I do not have plans," I say and take a breath. I continue, with hesitation. "And you have that play to go to, right?"

"Sure do. But I have an extra ticket if you want to join."

So here I am in the ninth hour of our first official date.

However, when I agreed to join him here, I didn't know he was actually going to be acting in the play. Well, technically, this is an improv theater show. He's one of the actors improvising tonight. This is exciting. The theater is small, seats for sixty-five people, but there is a bar, and Elijah is backstage, so the bar is about to be my friend while I wait for the show to start. Turn up—but not too much.

I order a whiskey ginger. Whiskey is my drink of autumn. Been this way since I started drinking legally at twenty-one. I scan the dim room and it's mostly Black and Brown folks here, and a sprinkle of *people who happen to be white*. I'm assuming they *happen to be white people* because all six of the ones I've counted are wearing some sort of shirt or pen with some social justice script or saying on it. One of them has a shirt saying "Dismantle Whiteness." I sometimes can vibe with *people who happen to be white* versus *white people*. I grew up with *white people*, but in college I met and became friends with three *people who happen to be white*. They understand their whiteness and use that knowledge to challenge it.

In my scanning, I notice someone who looks like Mario—my ex. Looks just like him, except this person has facial hair, a nice mustache and beard gracing his face. Mario was always smooth-faced and clean-cut. He's walking toward me. I look away and turn to face the bar because I don't want to look like a creeper.

"I told him that was you," he says, sliding next to my shoulder at the bar.

I look at him. It is Mario. I haven't seen him since Beyoncé and Jay-Z.

"Wow. I thought that was you! You look good. Different."

"Yeah, I decided to grow some facial hair this month," Mario says. "Starting No-shave November a week early. You look good, too. The same. A little heavier."

He giggles. The shade.

The lobby lights lower and the stage lights come on. People start to make their way back to their seats. I do not know what to do. I do not mind talking to Mario right now, and apparently he doesn't mind talking to me.

"Who are you here with?"

"I'm with Chris, one of my fraternity brothers," Mario says. "He's a transplant from the South. He asked me out and I thought why not. Feels kinda awkward, to be honest, but he's cute."

Oh. Mario's dating now. Hmm.

"Yeah, he looks like your type," I say, while looking over at Chris.

"Tall, dark, and handsome-ish?" Mario jokes again.

Something is light and free about Mario. Could it be that he's over me?

"You told him about me?" I ask.

"Yeah," Mario says. "I mean, everyone knew about you already. Even people you didn't know."

"Cool," I say, not really knowing what else to say. By now, the first actors are onstage, including Elijah.

"I'm here with him." I point to Elijah onstage.

"Seems to me you have a type, too."

"And what is that?" I ask, completely derailed because if Mario's alluding to the idea that he and Elijah resemble one another, I definitely cannot see it. Maybe their peanut butter complexion? Maybe. But other than that, I don't see it.

"He's cute," Mario says. "You like cute. And if they are smart, then that's a bonus. But you mostly just like cute."

He notices I'm not really feeling or getting the joke.

"What are you drinking?" Mario asks.

This should be obvious for him. There are few things that stay the same, and my seasonal drink of choice is one of them.

"Come on, you know what I'm drinking!"

I laugh.

"I do?" he says, completely surprised.

"It's autumn."

Mario is staring at me blankly. He is starting to shut down. He's losing interest in the small talk, the chitchat. To him this is banal. To me, this is a little thing that isn't little. We were together for years. I know he knows my autumn drink. Has he forgotten about me so soon?

"I'll have a tequila sunrise and another of whatever he ordered," Mario tells the bartender.

"That's a whiskey ginger, right?" the bartender asks and remembers.

"Yes. Whiskey. Ginger." I say it very slow and pointed toward Mario.

"Was that hard to say, whiskey ginger?" Mario asks.

"I thought you would have known," I rush out.

That was the first drink he made for me, the night we met.

"How was I supposed to know that's what you're drinking?"

I look around and notice we are the only ones at the bar. Chris is sitting, smiling over at us, with his perfect teeth, I'm sure waiting for Mario. Elijah is onstage glowing. And here I am, at the bar with someone I'm divorcing, borderlining anger, which is actually sadness, over the fact that the person I've spent most of my adult life with didn't know something so small, so little, yet, so big.

"Because it's autumn. That's how you were supposed to know."

I walk away from Mario, without taking the drink.

Mario walks to his seat and gives the drink—my whiskey ginger—to Chris, as if he really ordered it for him.

Kenny

ICYF: What About Your Friends?

It's been a few weeks since the Palms Spring trip, but now that I'm deep into my sessions with Thea the therapist, I figure it's as good a time as any to catch up with Carlos. One-on-one. I've got a vegan pizza with cauliflower crust baking in the oven, peppermint tea brewing on top of the stove, and a couple mugs sitting on the dining room table.

"Wow, and a fire in the fireplace, too," Carlos says after buzzing himself into the complex and opening my front door. "Someone's ready for cuffing season or just enjoying this gloomy, rainy weather today. What's up, Kenny?"

"I'm good, come here." I extend my arms and we hold each other in a tight, warm, auntie-like hug. "Missed you."

"Missed you, too."

"And definitely no cuffing season here, not with the work Thea the therapist got me doing," I say and disembark from Carlos, not because he and I aren't cuffing, but just because. It's in the mid-sixties outside, cold by L.A. standards. "It's just cold. I'm good, though. Tea?"

Carlos sits at the dining room while I pour the tea and get the pizza out the oven to cool. Will be a few minutes until it's edible, enough time for us to talk and catch up.

"Sorry I'm late, but I had a late meeting on campus—tell you more in a few," Carlos says and cups the warm mug in his hands.

"No prob. I've been here all day, trying to get this consulting work off the ground," I say. "This guy I met at my last DC gig wants to fly me out for a paid talk at the national convention for this organization called Brother Connection. So, I'm like I'll take it."

"Oh yeah, that," Carlos says. "Well, I'm really happy you called and invited me over. I spent the past few weeks trying to figure out if we're good, weird, or what."

"Oh, the whole 'Faith fucked the family' situation," I say, referring to both the nineties film *Soul Food* and the Palm Springs open relationship swapping. We chuckle. Comfort and familiarity between longtime friends. "We're good, Carlos."

"Of course we're good," Carlos says.

"Cool."

"Plus, the big Halloween carnival is coming up soon. Now Ricky and I got a place in WeHo to crash. Thanks for moving over here."

Over pizza, salad, and peppermint tea, we reminisce on the fact that a year ago at this time, we were collecting data and writing daily on our dissertations alongside our classmates Tyra and Lily, and slowly but surely trying to get to that April graduation finish line. We did, and I think of the joy of graduation and my mom, family, and friends watching me become Dr. Kane. A quick thought of what happened just a few days later—my mom's passing during my birthday week—slips in, but I switch up the thoughts to the joy I know she felt about my accomplishments.

But I also learn in our catch-up that Carlos and Ricky have officially evolved their fifteen-year relationship from monogamous to open-with-permission, and that the Palm Springs trip wasn't as big a deal to them as it was for Zaire and me. Not that I've been thinking of Zaire, or Preston, at all recently.

"And you're sure this is what makes you happy, Carlos?" I ask. I've known Carlos as long as he's known and been with Ricky. I know people are allowed to change, but I have never known Carlos to want anything but a one-man kinda man. "No judgment or anything. Just making sure you're…"

"We're fine, as long as it's mutual, consensual, and with the same person," Carlos says, sounding a bit defensive, but hey, not my call if Carlos isn't being one hundred with himself or with me. "I was the one who initiated with Alberto, anyway. I mean after you and Preston kept yourselves isolated up in the room together all day, leaving Alberto and Zaire by themselves."

I swivel hard toward Carlos's direction. "Left them by themselves?"

"Speaking of which, have you seen Alberto or Preston or Zaire lately?"

"Wait a minute, Carlos," I say. "You're taking Alberto's and Zaire's version of Palm Springs?"

"I mean, you invited them to my party and then barely socialized with anyone."

"Believe me, that's not my or Preston's version of events," I say. "But anyway, it doesn't matter now. I'm taking a break from that trio across the street. Therapy, remember? Thea the therapist."

Carlos walks over to the picture window to look across the street, and goes, "It must be so hard and so tempting to wanna see what's happening over there."

"Not really," I go. A small lie, but mostly truth. Therapy is working. "I mean, I'm more focused on healing me right now. Trying to stop repeating the same old shit."

"Gotcha. DaVon, Jeremy, Brandon-Malik, Zaire, all the others in between."

What's up with Carlos fucking with me, all of a sudden, I wonder.

"You trying to hold a mirror up to me or something?"

"No, not at all," he says. "I've made my mistakes. Granted, they haven't involved falling for full-of-bullshit Instagram models like Brandon-Malik, or little gangsta boys like Jeremy Lopez, but I've made them."

"I can tell you a few things about you, Carlos."

"I'm on your side, Kenny," Carlos says and makes his way back to the dining room area. He pours another cup of tea from the pot. "Just saying."

"Well then, stop saying, and let's change the subject," I say. "Because it sure sounds like you're trying to fuck with me."

"Fine," he goes. "And I'm not. Change the subject to what?"

"To anything but the mistakes and patterns I'm trying to work on," I say. "Thank you very much."

"What about grief and mourning? Is Thea the therapist helping you on that subject?"

"We're getting there, eventually," I say. "These boys-to-men situations—small shit. Before getting to the major shit of grief."

"Speaking of which, I know you're moving through grief," Carlos says and sips tea. "Before you say no, just say yes."

Carlos gets a grin on his face. This sounds like trouble. Or at minimum, something he knows I'm not going to be liking.

"What's up?" I say and then go, "I'm not saying yes or no until I hear what you've got to say."

"I think you'll like it. Kinda fits with what we've been talking about."

"Not a date. Please. I'm taking a hiatus from dating and romance."

"Nah, not a date," Carlos says and gets a bright smile on his face. He's up to something. I hope no more fuckery. "CUELA. They want you back on campus. *We* want you back."

I haven't given that place a thought since I emailed in my resignation letter from Ohio while handling funeral arrangements and clearing out my mom's house. He's got to be kidding, I think.

"You've got to be kidding," I say. "They want me back...now?"

"Yeah."

"In what role?"

"Assistant dean of students," Carlos says. "What do you think?"

So here's the fuckery I need to tell Thea the therapist about next time I see her. One more area to add to the list of issues to work through.

While I was away for six weeks on bereavement leave, the administrators at CUELA gave Carlos, my best friend and coworker for fifteen-plus years, temporary responsibility of my department, the diversity and inclusion unit on campus. When I submitted my resignation letter, because at the time I wasn't thinking about work, colleagues, or campus bureaucracy—only my mother and my two sisters and our family and how we were going to get everything that goes with losing your remaining parent done with peace, honor, and dignity—the next day, Carlos not only had a new title—dean of students—but he also had his department, my department, plus another area inherited from a colleague who chose to retire, under his professional umbrella.

Following my graduation and before the funeral, no one in the campus administration was talking to me at all about a promotion for me, though Carlos and I had the same years of experience, had just earned doctorate degrees together, and most of the ideas and initiatives he got credit for were ideas and initiatives from *my* area. Though he and I'd never talked, it made me wonder how long Carlos had been in discussion with administration about his advancement.

"Whose idea was this?" I ask.

"Well," Carlos starts. "I talked it over with the vice president—that was the meeting that made me late getting here—who gave the green light to ask if you'd be interested."

"But you're the dean of students."

"Right."

"And you're offering me assistant dean of students?"

"Yes," Carlos says and he's beaming. "We'd be a team again. Personally and professionally. The dynamic duo."

"Reporting to you."

"Of course."

"Reporting to you."

"I'm a good friend and an even better supervisor."

Carlos isn't getting it. So I decide to do something that I normally wouldn't do. Speak up.

"I'm insulted, Carlos."

"We're best friends."

"Exactly. And that's why I'm insulted that you'd come here with some bullshit offer like this."

"I'm confused."

"I turned down an associate vice president job at a community college," I say. "You know this. I told you."

"But then you started the consulting and presentations thing, and I thought your rightful place was back at CUELA where we made everything happen."

"Where *I* made everything happen," I say and continue, "and you and everyone else got the credit and accolades. I should be the fucking vice president or higher at that place, everyone on campus says it and knows it. And you come here with assistant dean. To report to *you*? My best friend?"

"I didn't think it was gonna be this big a deal," Carlos says. "We all want you back at CUELA."

"What were the first three words you just said?"

"I didn't think…"

"Exactly," I say. "You didn't think."

"You do your own share of not thinking, Kenny," Carlos says. "And I'm there for you always. Through all your dumb and disappointing mistakes. Brandon-Malik. Zaire and Preston. Jeremy Lopez. DaVon…"

"Right, DaVon," I say. "Thanks to you and Ricky."

"I can't believe you're upset with me offering you a job. You're doing nothing with your life now but living on insurance money, doing a so-called consulting business and I don't see much business by the way, going to therapy about boys that are not worth your time when you really should be focusing on the fact that your mom died and you're avoiding dealing with that."

"Are you done, Carlos?" I ask. "And you can leave my mom out of this. You didn't even come to Ohio for the funeral, and I told you how much it would have meant for me to have you there."

"I'm sorry. Something came up at work, like graduation season at CUELA," Carlos says. "And for the record, I was on FaceTime or messaging you every day when you were out, unlike some people who ghosted you and broke up with you via text and you're still trying to get him back in your life. That's bright, Dr. Kane."

"Bright like you and Ricky all of a sudden having an open relationship?"

"Irrelevant to this conversation," Carlos says. "And I never got a thanks for taking on all your work and your department and your responsibilities while you were out."

"Well, thank you now and fuck you, Carlos. And tell whatever administrators you're kissing up to lately to take the bullshit offer to be your assistant and to stuff it where the sun don't shine."

The room is tense. We've never really had a fight, but I am pissed because I am hurt. Therapy taught me that. To feel and to express it. And I am not done.

"You know, Carlos," I say. "Moments like these, I remember you're white."

"I'm *Mexican*!"

"And?"

"So you're going there?" Carlos asks. "It's like that then?"

"Yeah, it's like that."

He gathers up his phone, work bag, and starts to pick up the tea mug.

"Don't touch that. I got it."

"Well, it breaks my heart that you think I'm not on your side, Kenny," Carlos says. "When I've been there for you more than anyone else in L.A. since you moved here all those years ago."

"You've got a fine way of showing it."

"I love you, but you make it hard for me to like you. Most of the time, but definitely right now."

"The feeling is mutual."

"Then I'm out."

"Don't stop on my account."

Carlos stands in the open door frame and stares at me, "So this is how we part, Kenny?"

"Bye."

Carlos walks out without closing the door. I walk over and slam it shut.

Assistant. My ass.

Kenny

ICYF: Find Home and Go

Packed a bag and caught an overnight flight. Now I'm in the land of flat and fat—Ohio. Toledo, to be exact.

It's a little after six in the morning Midwest time, and it's too late to call or text anyone on the West Coast to let them know that I've landed—not that I've got anyone to call or text at the moment there. And it's too early to call or text anyone in the Midwest that I'm home for a bit. A surprise visit. Just felt like getting out of L.A. and going somewhere that feels familiar. Like home.

I haven't been back to Ohio in five months since my sisters and I were making arrangements, coordinating family travel and schedules, and then clearing out my mom's house. Thea the therapist is gradually moving me into the work of grieving, now that I've been pretty successful in weaning myself off of the low-hanging fruit of my life—Brandon-Malik, Alberto, Preston, and Zaire. So I figured, what the hell? No man, no friends, no job (except for the upcoming DC Brother Connection convention gig), no need to stick around all that nothingness.

This is not a pity party. That's what Thea the therapist would say.

I get on the automatic walkway in the airport and just stand. Nothing to do and all day to do it. I take my time deciding if I'm going to the car rental center, catching a Lyft or Uber, getting a hotel room, or waiting for a few hours until it's a decent hour to call, text, and say, "Surprise, your brother, uncle, cousin is in town, who's taking me in?"

In the meantime, I'm taking in the businesspeople dressed in boring blue suits, conservative haircuts, thick waistlines, and pasty pink skin. I forgot how white-white it is in Ohio. Like everywhere white. And as blah as the cloudy, overcast sky that I see peeking through the windows while I glide through the airport hallway. I'm being mean. I'm sleepy. And I'm mean.

After a ten-minute lazy stroll through the airport, I find the car rental—Hertz. I make it all the way to the front of the line and decide to call a Lyft instead. I am in no condition to be behind heavy machinery, figuring out these Toledo highways and streets after so many years of not living here. Not the way my brain is hopping around from thought to thought, from feel to feel. I go to the back of the rental car room and sit with my one bag. I get out my phone and go to my sister Cecily's contact to get her address, then I go to my sister Tonya's contact to get her address. I open the Lyft app and place both of their addresses in to see who is closest to the airport, because whoever is closest to the airport is the person I do *not* want to stay with today, because when I get this Lyft I want the drive to be as long as it can be. This will allow me to clear more of my brain before I'm with family.

I'm thankful my Lyft driver is cute and of color—he's one of those exotically Black types that would do well in commercial Hollywood, and would definitely be popular with the men in West Hollywood. Maybe this is a sign that the day will get better.

"Good morning, Kenny!" Lyfty greets me.

"Morning, Monte." I give a dry response.

"You only have one bag, so I take it you're returning back home."

I'm usually a great morning person. But this morning I'd rather sit and be in my own thoughts in my own head, on my own. Besides, it's still four in the morning in L.A., and to be honest, I'm never up at four in the morning. Maybe 4:30, but never just four.

"I guess you can say that."

I put on my Beats to signal to Monte that I do not wish to talk right now.

❖

Thank goodness Tonya lives in a subdivision adjacent to the airport, and Cecily lives farther, in a wannabe warehouse and arts district near downtown and closer to the water.

I choose Cecily's place to crash at. She won't mind me just showing up without notice and blending into the chaos of her warehouse-slash-living-slash-art space. Fits with her personality. I'm sure by now she and Akili are up, getting the tweens ready for the weekend African Academy school they run, and getting their steel oats and flax/chia seed green smoothies ready for breakfast. That's my speed. She's the cool cat, and the youngest, of the Kane crew. Afrocentric. Creative. Open-minded. Organic. All that. She and Naija the therapist would be besties, if they ever met. I can't believe she's thriving in Toledo, of all places, after living in the Bay Area for so many years after college.

At one point in our lives, all of us Kanes escaped the Midwest and were living on the West Coast.

Cecily, the youngest, and her husband Akili, college sweethearts, operated an African art store and artist space in Oakland. Even with infant twins, Cecily and Akili threw the biggest and most eclectic Pride events for people of color in San Francisco and Oakland, until gentrification forced them out of home and business and back to Toledo. Tonya Kane-Montgomery, the middle, and her husband Michael Montgomery—more like power partners—lived a storybook life in Phoenix for the longest time— she, a trained nurse, who opted to be stay-at-home mother, and he, the number one news anchor—and only Black anchor in Phoenix at the time—did nothing but make money, spend money, and raise my two little Black Miss America nieces. And my mom lived with me for almost five years in my suburban L.A. home when she was separating and divorcing her second husband. She took up Tonya's offer to live with her family in Toledo, when Michael got an offer as lead anchor and news director of the local CBS affiliate there. Convenient. Mom missed her hometown, Toledo.

Now our mom is gone. I'm home, again. The sadness floods back—the family's L.A. visit during my graduation season, the Kane family pride in my becoming a doctor, then a week later… I should have called Thea the therapist before making this spontaneous trip home. I'm going to miss our next appointment and I'll probably need her.

❖

My Lyft drops me off in front of Cecily's place and I see that she, Akili, and the twins are heading out to their weekend errands. It's foggy and I feel silly for forgetting how chilly it is in Ohio right before Halloween. I probably look foolish in a denim jacket with no hat, gloves, or scarf. They've all got on puffy coats and hats.

"Hey, Ceci," I call out. "Don't y'all leave without me."

"Brother? Doctor! Is that you?" Cecily runs over to the Lyft and jumps up in the air. She's excited. "Get the fuck out. You're in Toledo? Did you bring Brandon-Malik?"

Damn. I forgot she and the family met and loved—I mean LOVED—Brandon-Malik at my graduation and graduation party back in late April. I forgot I haven't told the family that Brandon-Malik and I are not together anymore, nor the circumstances behind me and him not being together.

"Not this time," I say. Nothing else to say right now, anyway, but eventually, I will say.

"Aww, damn," Cecily says. "He's cool people. We all loved us some Brandon-Malik."

"But you have your brother," I say, smile, and open up my arms and spirit fingers.

Though I am sleepy, still, from an overnight flight and on 5 a.m. L.A. time now, I join in my sister's enthusiastic hugs. It multiplies when her twins—my twin niece and nephew, Nia and Amen—run toward me and join in the love circle.

"You're going to school with us, right, Uncle Kenny?" Nia and Amen say in unison. At twelve, it appears they're still inseparable and still replicate what the other says. They're such joy. Innocent and young Black joy. "Amen and I are giving a talk today about the matriarchal societies of Africa and how toxic Black masculinity in the U.S. negates our African roots. Wanna watch?"

I look at Cecily and Akili, who's picked up my bag, with a "what the fuck are you teaching these brilliant young people" look, and go, "Of course I will go."

"Yay!" my niece and nephew go in unison. "We'll bring up the Prezi on our tablets when Mom and Dad are driving. Sit in the back with us so you can help us rehearse again."

"Definitely."

"We put pictures of Grandma in the Prezi," Nia offers. And Amen continues, "It keeps the spirit of the ancestors alive."

These kids are brilliant and woke. And I forget about my sleepiness and wake up.

❖

While we're weaving through the mostly empty streets—it's Saturday morning—Cecily and Akili offer up some of the latest happenings with the Kane family in Ohio. I haven't been in town more than a few hours, but it already feels like home again. And I haven't even been home yet per se—to Cecily's, Tonya's, or Mom's old place.

This is the part of L.A./West Hollywood life that we don't get to see or share with each other. Since many of us are transplants of some sort—whether we've moved to L.A. to pursue dreams, or run away from family issues, or create a new life where we can be 100 percent our whole queer selves—we don't know who each of our friends, neighbors, or club acquaintances really are. Just the front we put on, the image we create, the people we pretend to be.

No one knows about who we were before our L.A. lives— favorite teachers, the smells associated with our parents' or grandparents' homes, sibling rivalries and relationships, first crushes and prom dates, favorite meals, experiencing a change of seasons, chores we were assigned and hated or loved, raking leaves, shoveling snow, walks to the corner candy store, bike rides with neighborhood best friends, church life, awards and certificates for hobbies we don't do anymore, holiday traditions and favorite gifts, and more—the memories, experiences, and things who make us who we really are.

Here, in Toledo, riding through the neighborhood with my sister, her husband, and kids, I know they know me, love me, accept me. I don't have to pretend to be anyone else but Kenny Kane, older brother and uncle. Granted, no one here knows yet about the work I'm doing with Thea the therapist. And I have yet to tell them about Brandon-Malik's disappearance from my life and how that, in combination with losing Mom, has sent me on a journey like no other.

I have an aha moment amidst the journey through Toledo on this weekend morning. Getting home is important for me. To get back to a place of remembering who, what, and where we're from is important.

❖

Sometime during the morning African Academy, Cecily and Tonya touch base, then Tonya and I touch base, and Tonya touches base with all of us at the same time. Tonya invites us all over to her place, which is where we're heading right now, after a quick trip to the cemetery where Mom is. My duty, obviously, this short trip home. See Mom.

It's a little before three and I have yet to shower, change clothes, brush my teeth, or get the L.A. and airplane stench off me. It's okay, though, because seeing Nia, Amen, and all their little Afrocentric classmates during optional Saturday school is refreshing and makes me forget all of the superficial details of grooming that consume me daily in L.A. But I will groom and freshen up once we get to Tonya's place.

Where Tonya and her husband and kids live is a place where we only dreamed of as kids while growing up in our working-class part of Toledo. Tonya's in the "rich part of town" now, where it's gated most of the year except for Halloween, when working-class parents are allowed to accompany their kids to trick-or-treat for the so-called "good candy," and the winter holiday season, when big houses and luscious lawns are covered with all sorts of holiday lights, real or fake snow, and larger-than-life figurines.

As we walk up the long driveway, we see Tonya's husband Michael on a tall ladder that's perched next to one of the pillars that remind me of the White House. Yeah, they live in that kind of house.

Nia and Amen rush ahead of us, eager to play with their older cousins, Tory and Micah.

"Stop running," Cecily calls out, demonstrating her fiercest Black mama skills that she often shares as a guest on the *Dem Black Mamas* podcast. The kids slow down. "We all going to the same place."

"Hey, Michael," I say, seeing deflated winter holiday decorations strewn over the front yard. Certainly, with all the money he makes, he could pay a crew of workers to do the yearly lights, but one thing I know for sure—he and Tonya stay rich because they're frugal. "It's not even Halloween yet."

"Kenny! Sup, y'all," Michael yells. "Go on in. Tonya's in there. I'm just trying to get the Christmas lights up before it gets too cold and snowy."

"I got you, Mike," Akili yells back and heads toward Michael, the ladder, and multiple strings of lights. "As long as you return the favor next weekend at the warehouse, brother."

"Most def," Michael yells. "We'll be in in about an hour."

Before the front door can fully shut, Nia and Amen are running to the upstairs bedrooms to find Tory and Micah. Tonya descends the same grand staircase the kids are running up, ever the diva with her flowing honey-blond Beyoncé tresses and golden caftan-style dress.

"Hey, brother. Hey, sister. Let's make our way to the kitchen."

She always been so damn formal, like we're on one of those HGTV, Food Channel, Better Home and Gardens shows she likes to watch while Michael is at work, and while her Tory and Micah are in school. Cecily and I give each other that look, roll our eyes, and almost giggle as we *make our way* through Tonya's enormous house.

The kitchen smells like Sunday dinner on a Saturday, which excites me. Since arriving in the morning, all I've had was remnants of Cecily's green smoothie. I'm starving.

"Smells good in here, Tonya," I say. "What's cooking?"

"All of our favorites from Mom's freezer and kitchen… but before we eat," Tonya opens up her hands and arms over the massive kitchen island like she's a model on *The Price Is Right*, "let's do shots."

"Shots?" Cecily asks at the same time I do.

"Shots."

"I ain't ate all day, Tonya," I say. "And I could still use a shower, if you don't mind me using one of the extra bathrooms."

"You're with family, brother," Tonya says, and pours three dark liquor shots. "We don't care about your smell, and you shouldn't. We're just glad you're here. Cheers."

I choke back the shot that tastes like Hennessy and we all make that sound like we've just resuscitated ourselves with fresh air once we've swallowed.

"Alexa, play playlist Auntie Jams," Tonya says, and Chaka Khan's voice soars in surround sound glory through the kitchen.

"How dope," I go. Like clockwork, Tonya and Cecily chime in like Whitney did at the end of her version of *I'm Every Woman*. "Chaka Khan."

"Remember your wedding," I say and point to Tonya, "when Mom got tipsy…okay, drunk…and started lip-syncing and acting out this song on the dance floor?"

"I was so embarrassed, but we had fun," Tonya says. "Mom was fun…and funny."

"And didn't take no shit," Cecily says, pours herself another shot, and before downing it says, "Oooh child, the ghetto. Akili's driving, thank goodness."

"Everyone can crash here tonight," Tonya says. "We've got plenty of bedrooms and space. It'd be like old times."

"You've changed, Tonya," I say. "That's a good thing."

"Have I...yeah, maybe," Tonya says. "We all know why. Mama. Still can't believe she's gone."

"I know, right," Cecily says. "When you're growing up, you think your parents are gonna be here forever. They're like immortal beings."

"Since the funeral, I've been trying to loosen up, let this librarian bun down, so to speak," Tonya says. "I've been such an uptight bitch, pardon my cussing. I don't want my kids to remember me that way."

"Remember me different," I go, and we all laugh, thinking about that one episode of *Insecure* with the character Kelly and her antics at Coachella. "That show. I swear. My life."

Cecily goes, "You're the Molly of your group, huh, Kenny?"

"I take offense," I say, thinking about the *Insecure* character Molly, a success in her professional and academic life, a mess in her personal and romantic life. "But it's true."

"What's going on, Kenny?" Tonya asks. She's never really been warm to anything related to my personal life, especially anything related to my gay personal life. Obviously, Mom's death has us all in some kind of way. "And why didn't you bring that guy who was at your graduation party in L.A.?"

"I asked about Brandon-Malik this morning when Kenny got here," Cecily chimes in. Feels like I'm about to be tag-teamed. "And you ain't tell me nothing. Brandon-Malik is fine."

"If I wasn't a married woman," Tonya says, "I'd be the first to say that Brandon-Malik could get it. With his young twenty-seven-year-old self."

"You're my sisters," I say. "I don't like hearing you all talk like this. And you're just ten years older than him, Tonya."

I pour another shot and sip it slowly. I'm feeling warm. We

haven't eaten yet. I'm probably gonna get drunk. Tonight. In Toledo, Ohio. With my family.

"What's up with bae?" Cecily asks and pulls out her phone to scroll through pictures from my April graduation celebration. She holds up a picture of Brandon-Malik and me, in all my academic regalia, taken right after the commencement ceremony ended. "He's all Mama could talk about when we got back to Toledo. 'Kenny got a fine man,' 'Oooh, child, that Brandon-Malik and Kenny make a cute couple,' 'Kenny's little friend needs to meet the rest of the family in Ohio, because I want them married.'"

"Mama was happy for you, Kenny," Tonya says. "And proud. You're her favorite, you know."

"Stop," I say, trying to hold back a few tears—not just for Mom, but also for what I haven't shared yet about Brandon-Malik. "She said that really?"

"Mmm-hmm," Cecily says.

I can't. So I go, "Can we eat soon?"

"We'll eat soon enough, I'm hungry, too," Tonya says. "But you don't come home enough for us to know about your day-to-day."

"So what's up with bae?" Cecily asks again. "Why didn't he come home with you?"

I'm buzzed, hungry, and still dirty from the overnight flight and hanging all day, so I might as well come clean. So I go, "Brandon-Malik dumped me."

"What?"

"Mmmmmm, no way!"

"Yeah. Long story short, he couldn't be there for me after Mom died." I go and grab a nearby napkin because I'm going to lose it, despite the fact that I've been working on myself with Thea the therapist and have been okay with the reality that Brandon-Malik and I are a thing of the past. "I didn't tell y'all this, but he texted me for the first time right before Mom's funeral that he was sorry for not calling or checking in on us…"

Tonya whips around that honey-blond hair, much like she used to do her then jet-black hair, when we were kids and pissed off at something, and says, "You mean after he hung out with our family for the two weeks we were in L.A. for your graduation, ate and drank on Mom's dime like every night and especially at your graduation party at the top of the Bonaventure...he just stopped being there for you when our mother died?"

"That was a week after your graduation...fucker," Cecily chimes in. She mad, too. "And your birthday week...asshole."

"Well, might as well tell you everything," I say. "So after I got to Toledo and while we were in the limo to the funeral, Brandon-Malik texts me this Aaliyah four-page-letter text about how he's sorry he couldn't be there for me, he's never been in the situation of supporting someone in mourning, blah blah blah."

"Grown people figure that shit out how to support people," Tonya says. "There is no road map. Unless you're an emotionless psychopath, narcissist, or something."

"At first, I was like...I get it," I go. "But really, I didn't get it. Not after all I'd done with and for Brandon-Malik. And I did a *lot* that I'm not even going to get into, because you'll both be trying to get flights to L.A. tonight to find him."

"Bet you didn't know this," Cecily says. "Mom said she gave him a grand in L.A. because he gave her some sob story about not being able to get you a suitable graduation gift. He took her on a drive to the bank while we were doing some touristy shit or something with the kids. She told me."

"She did?" Tonya and I say simultaneously. I'm definitely shocked at Mom's generosity with Brandon-Malik, and shocked that Cecily knew this and never said anything to me before.

"I woulda thought he'd use that money, or at least have some of it left, to fly back with you for Mom's funeral, seeing that everything happened so fast," Cecily says. "You ain't say nothing about him not having steady work."

"He works," I say. Can't believe I'm coming to his defense, just a little. "When he gets a gig. It's L.A., he's trying to make it as a model, you know."

"He don't have a job, Kenny?" Tonya asks.

"Well..."

"Tonya, remember me telling you about my girl Antoinette, and the man/boy from Detroit she met online?" Cecily asks and purses her lips.

"That kinda work?" Tonya goes. "Oh hell naw, Kenny. In case you forgot, you know Mama felt a way about a man not having job. And trying to be with one of us? And you're a doctor?"

Cecily goes, "An Instagram model, stylist, personal coach and trainer ain't work. I know about that pretty boy bullshit. It's code word for 'ain't doing shit.' They travel, shop, work out all day, every day, but you never see or hear anything about work. That's trifling."

My phone buzzes, my first notification of the day since traveling from L.A. to Toledo. See, I really don't have friends since the blow-up with Carlos or going on the ninety-day breakup detox from Thea the therapist. Subject line says *Zaire's 30th*, but I'm not answering or responding...not with the Kane sisters on my case about Brandon-Malik right now.

"So you've just been carrying this for almost six months?" Tonya says, crosses the island to be near me, and puts her arms around my shoulders.

Cecily joins. "Poor brother."

"Don't 'poor Kenny' me," I say. "I've been in therapy. Trying to work through this year. It's been a lot."

"Of course," Tonya says. "We all lost Mom. But you don't have to go through this all alone. None of us has to."

Cecily pats my shoulder.

"You could just move back home and be with family again," she says. "Besides, you were a natural today at the kids' Saturday school. Put that doctorate to work with your own people in your hometown. Black kids—Black people period—need accessible role models in their own neighborhood."

"I'm sure Michael can get you something at the TV station. If you wanted. My days of dictating and ordering around are over, in case you haven't noticed."

Tonya heads back toward the stovetop, where our mom's food is heating up. I see and smell fried corn, collard greens, sweet potatoes, and dressing. All foods that my mom would cook in batches and then freeze up for the winter. I'm glad she did that. It's like Mom is cooking for us today.

"But first, another shot?" Cecily goes.

"Dinner?" I say.

We laugh. I love being with my sisters.

❖

After three too many shots, neither Cecily, Akili, or I were in the mood or shape to try and drive back to Cecily's, so crashing at Tonya's place we are.

It's three in the morning and I'm in one of Tonya's spare bedrooms on the third floor of her home. Alternating between staring at the ceiling and staring out the bedroom window. Being home with my sisters is therapeutic. However, eating Mom's food for dinner, being so close to where she lived most of her life and is now buried, has me thinking. Not in a bad way. Just the nighttime way. Nighttime is worst for reflecting and wondering.

My phone chimes. New text. I reach over to the nightstand to see what and who would want to contact me at this time of night.

Was just thinking about that time we went to the Drake concert. That was a good date. Our best date. I love you. B.

Vomit.

Brandon-Malik. As if I don't know what the *B* stands for in a text from him.

I can't fucking believe it. Mostly because I never even responded to his *hi* text all those months ago. He must be drunk, it's around midnight in L.A. I'm sure he's at one of the bars in West Hollywood tonight. *I love you* means nothing with whiskey on the breath, though.

I need another shot, though I don't need another shot. But I get out of bed to walk around the house.

When I get to the kitchen, I turn on the lights and see Tonya sitting alone at the island with a glass of wine in front of her.

"Shit, you scared me," I go. "What's bothering you, Tonya?"

"Nothing. Just thinking. Mama." She sips from the wine glass. "Why are you up at three in the morning?"

"Honest?"

"Any other way?" She takes another sip.

"I just got a text from Brandon-Malik out of the blue," I say. "So I came to get a shot. I'll have wine instead."

"Glasses in the cabinet by the fridge," Tonya says.

"Get one for me, too," Cecily says and clears her throat. She's joined us in the kitchen. She must be thinking, too. The three of us up at three. Damn. "And give me your phone, Kenny."

"Nah, sis," I say. "It's cool, thanks. I have this one handled. I think."

Zaire and The JamesGang

ICYF: Laissez Les Bons Temps Rouler

Zaire

Halloween in the gayborhood is epic. Too epic. You'd think because it was during the week this year, the party would have turned down a little. Nope, not in this town.

It's my birthday today. Thank goodness I didn't drink so much on Halloween, or else I'd still be recovering like my roommate Alberto. Poor guy. He should have joined me in having one of the cannabis transdermal aka weed skin patches that my brother Harlem provided. Alberto's been hungover for over two days, but this morning he seems much better, and he looks like he'll make my thirtieth birthday party after all.

I'm so happy I did not have to plan a damn thing for this party. The year I've had, I would have been okay bringing in the dirty thirty watching old movies and eating popcorn. But a party also sounded fun, especially now that I'm actually enjoying music and life again.

Ever the planner and organizer, Savannah insisted we celebrate with an over-the-top party. I have a feeling she's making it a big deal because it'll give her a goal to try and top today's party for her thirtieth next year. I heard through the grapevine that she called all of her Greek-letter Divine Nine elites and party planners and got the festivities together in two weeks. All she asked for were the contacts of all of my closest friends in my phone—I just gave it to her, for some sense of surprise.

I am sitting on the edge of my hotel bed in an all-black slim-fitted suit that Savannah purchased from Nordstrom. I'm enjoying my last few moments of solo time before I have to go downstairs to the ballroom for the grand thirtieth New Orleans–style masquerade. Savannah informed me to make an entrance, so I'm taking my sweet time arriving.

I sent Elijah the party information via text a few days ago. He is the only person I want to make sure is at my celebration. He said he wouldn't promise he'd make it because he had plans with his actor friends for their social consciousness group meeting, a commitment he made a few days before my invite. He wanted to know why I hadn't told him sooner, and I lied and said that I didn't have all of the details, given that Savannah was planning everything. The truth is, I'm not sure I'm ready for him to meet my family. I'm not sure if I want him to meet my friends. I just am not sure if I want him to bring in this new chapter and decade of my life with me and with the people I love most.

Despite my hesitancy, I must admit I am a bit bummed about Elijah not giving me a definite answer of coming. I wanted him to drop all his plans for my party. Even if I had given him a short notice. Then I thought some more and realize it's actually wonderful of him to not drop something for me, especially because we have just started dating. I mean, he's being honest and communicating. Some dudes would have said they'd be there for sure, flake, and then give the truth later.

I take one final puff off my pen and put on these new Ted Baker Chelsea boots—another Savannah purchase—and stand in the mirror thinking *this is thirty*. For a split second I think about last year's birthday, and how Mario gave me a surprise brunch at some fancy Hollywood place, where the food was too expensive, servings too small, and mimosas too weak. I thought about how I wanted to go to see *A Bronx Tale* play instead of a fancy brunch with a bunch of *his* friends, the ones I wasn't really friends with.

I smile at myself in the mirror because I can see how much I've changed physically and emotionally this year. I take a couple of mirror selfies and send them to Elijah. I walk out of my room, turning off all of the lights, except for a dim, sexy light near my bed. I mean, you never know. The birthday boy is coming down…Let's see what Savannah's got planned for the evening!

Savannah

The party is going to be wonderful. This I know.

It's been my main priority for the past two months. Let Zaire tell it, he'll say I've been planning for two weeks. But little does he know, I've been planning without his knowledge all along, right after the intervention brunch I pulled together. Originally, I wanted to give him a surprise birthday party, but after thinking about the year he's had —the job change, the move, and the divorce—I figured he probably wouldn't fully appreciate another surprise. So, two and half weeks ago I *asked* if I could plan a party for his thirtieth.

I just can't wait for it to be over. I'm big as a house and anxious. But this isn't about me, this is about my older brother and his party. It's really going to be great.

All I need is for everyone to show up on time and have a good time. Everything is paid. All of the decorations are up and perfect—I assembled the best events crew I know. I met the band a couple of days ago to have them rehearse in front of me because their online experience was good, but it wasn't enough for me. I needed to hear them live to rest my nerves. I've scheduled the cake to arrive in about an hour. Yes, only one hour before the party! I can't stand a cake that's been out and ready all day. Speaking of the cake, it's gorgeous—I designed it, well, visioned it. The cake is three tiers of moist marble deliciousness in the shape of a fleur-de-lis. One of my sorority sisters had her sister from Compton bake and assemble it. Even though I've got means, I have no qualms going to the hood for excellent gems for cheaper prices.

It is the least I can do. I love my brother even if I do not show it often. I really appreciate who he is and who he's been to our little family. He truly has kept us together over the years. And I haven't done my part in showing how much I appreciate his stubborn self.

This pregnancy is teaching me to show my love more. I'm thankful for the baby already for this. Who knew it would take an accidental pregnancy for me to learn how to express my love for my brother? By accidental, I mean, I wanted a child with Anthony, but I was aiming more toward after I turned the big 3-0. I should have followed my sister Langston's lead and got the IUD. But there's no need to fuss about spilled milk seven months in; what's done is happening, and it's a blessing. I think I'm going to have the middle name be Zai, as a gift for my brother Zaire. The name Zai sounds nice and is gender neutral enough. Yeah, Zai will be little baby's middle name.

I've spent the night and today at the same hotel as the party, so I can go back and forth to my room if need be. Langston braided my hair a couple days ago and put it in a nice high bun. Danielle, my line sister, has beat my face so good that I'm ready for a photo shoot. Now all I have to do is slip my sexy pregnant self into this short black dress. My stomach may be big as infinity, but my legs are nice and thick. So I must show them off. And the girls on top are looking good, too. Before the pregnancy I was a 34B, now I'm a 36C. Anthony loves them, and I love that he loves them.

Anthony has just gotten out of the shower. He's drying off in front of me and looking like a sexy Hershey's bar. Get it, big-daddy-to-be. Langston is on her way to my suite to get dressed. Harlem should be arriving soon. Everyone should be in the ballroom, as instructed, before the birthday boy. I specifically told everyone in their invitations to be here at eight o'clock post meridiem, sharp!, so that my big brother, Zaire E. James, can have a proper entrance after everyone else's arrival.

Everyone RSVP'd. Which is a shocker for Black folks. Everyone knows Zaire has had a year.

I feel horrible not inviting Mario, Zaire's ex, or soon-to-be-ex-husband. I actually cried about it to Anthony. Mario has been a part of our family for years and has been to many of our family celebrations. I asked Harlem who in Mario and Zaire's couple circle I should invite, and he told me everyone except Mario. That made me even more sad. Divorces are the worst. I asked Harlem if Zaire was talking to anyone special that I should invite, and he told me about this older guy named Kenny. Apparently Kenny is the neighbor guy he's been talking to. I didn't probe much more because I trust Harlem's insights.

I'm pretty sure I'm going to be the only sober one at the party tonight—pregnancy, you know. I may take a little fake sip on some Martinelli's during the toast that I wrote for Langston to deliver on our family's behalf.

My yoga for mommies classes has paid off because it's 6 p.m. and I'm fully energized to get down. Let the good times roll or, as Pawpaw used to say, "Laissez les bons temps rouler!"

Let's hope Zaire enjoys what I've done for him.

Zaire

The band is showing off tonight. All of my friends are here, even people I haven't seen all year. Even folks from Mario's circle have decided to party with us tonight. This is surprising, and another reason I'm thrilled I didn't have to plan this party. I would have struggled to figure out who to invite and who *not* to invite. Ever since the separation and my move out, I do not know who I can actually talk to—especially the so-called friends in Mario's circle. I met many BlaQueer socialites via Mario, and when it became public knowledge that Mario and I were over—when I got on the hook-up apps, and people started hitting me up as to why I'm on them—I figured that all of the relationships I formed through Mario would end, too.

Leave it to Savannah to invite them anyway, and they are all here. I'm surprised. It feels a little weird to see so many of Mario's circle, especially when I made my grand entrance, but everyone has nothing but smiles and hugs and cheers for me. Can I turn thirty again next year?

The dance floor hasn't felt alone all night! Savannah has outdone herself! Go Savannah! After my fifth dance to all the bops, I take my sweaty ass to the head table reserved for me and take another view of all the people here. My Auntie Sharon—my mother's younger and only sibling—is dancing with all the queer bois, and she's mastering the latest dance moves. She can easily pass for my sister. Well, maybe an older sister, as she's about twenty years my senior but doesn't look a day over thirty-five. That's good Black. She's the cool auntie everyone deserves.

All of my daddy's people are here, too. I am glad they remember us and still stay in touch, even though Dad's been gone for years. My first and favorite cousin Will came with his three kids who are all under ten, and they are running around playing with the other kids. I enjoy the sight of kids at the party. Apparently, Savannah told everyone that although it would be kid-welcoming, adult partying would partake, and that the parents would have to be parents and take care of their own kids.

I continue taking in all of the love in this grand ballroom. It feels good to be surrounded by so many smiles tonight.

There's only one person who seems a bit out of place. No one else notices because no one else can see what I see. Kenny looks sooooo not present at his table, and it looks like he's at a table with my coworker Jada and her bae Chris, plus some of Mario's socialites who may be on Kenny's level. But Kenny doesn't look like he's really enjoying himself. If I know Kenny at all, he's probably all in his head and questioning why he even showed up. We haven't spoken about my disappearing act since Palm Springs or our little back-and-forth dating, not dating, arguing, not arguing. He's probably reliving our situation, as I sit here feeling good.

Tonight, I want everyone, *everyone*, to be happy. Too much sadness in this sad world, so tonight, I don't want to be sad or mad or anything less than high. As in high off life. Or weed. Whatever is currently working best. Which somewhat reminds me, I shouldn't have another drink. The goal of my dirty-thirty grand party is simple. I want people vibing.

I told myself that at thirty, I'm going to act different. Whatever that means. Such an arbitrary thing to say at an arbitrary number. I'm going to be an adult always and face what needs to be faced, or whatever. So here I go, on my way walking confidently to talk to Kenny.

"You look nice Mr. K—I mean, Dr. Kane," I say to Kenny. "Would you like to dance?"

Kenny gets up from the table and links arm with me. The band has slowed the music down, thanks to my request right before heading Kenny's way.

"Can you loosen up, it looks like you've seen a ghost," I whisper in his ear as we sway back and forth.

He clears his throat and slightly exhales. "Well, um, I'm sorry."

I know he'll be stressing about that *sorry* all night. If he's going to stress all night, why even come? I'm trying to think about how Savannah put Kenny on the list. Or which one of my siblings did. Let me put this man out of this misery.

"Oh, Kenny," I say. "You're so weird."

"What you mean?"

I say nothing.

"And you're weird?" Kenny continues.

Yay! He remembers. We are weird together.

"You don't have to be sorry," I say. "What happened between you and that heaux Preston is spilled and spoiled milk."

I say this, hoping that would do the trick of making him feel a little better about being here, given we haven't talked about that weekend.

He leans his head back so we are face-to-face. He squints his eyes. We are rocking back and forth looking at each other in the face. Everyone seems to disappear in the moment. Kenny is handsome and tender.

"And I'm sorry," I say, forcing his head back to my neck area.

"What are you sorry about, Zaire?" he whispers in my ear.

I am not sure if I have the words to share. Lies. I am not sure if I really want to admit what I'm sorry about. But, I remember, at thirty I'm going to be better.

"I'm sorry for being a mess. For sending you all them *what you doin?* texts during ungodly hours, knowing full well the only thing open during that time of night are legs and twenty-four-hour McDonald's drive-through windows, which is really saying—bad decisions. I'm sorry for leading you on all those times."

I hear a sniffle in my ear. I lean back to see him wipe a tear from his face. Have I said something wrong? Leading him on was harsh. I feel horrible. But I was still figuring things out with my divorce, the apps, fucking around, trying to date again. Hell, I'm still figuring it out. But at least I'm admitting my faults now. At thirty, I got to get my shit together. I have to make amends and mend the things that I can.

"I didn't mean to make you cry, Kenny." I struggle to find the words to respond to Kenny's show of emotions.

"You didn't," he says. "You really are sweet, Zaire. A little unpredictable and inconsistent, but sweet and kind underneath it all."

A little unpredictable and inconsistent? Well, damn. Read me on my birthday. At *my* birthday party.

"Thanks. I guess?" I giggle.

The song is finishing up and I hope he is feeling a little less tense. The photographer is taking candid pictures of everyone. I cannot have Kenny looking unpleasant in one more damn picture during my birthday party. I see through his fake smiles. The eyes give it away. The eyes always give it away.

"Can I walk you back to your table?" I ask.

Kenny looks back at the table. And shit! Alberto and Preston have apparently arrived with a guest, and the two of them are now getting up to dance. The other guy with my roommate and his heaux, whose name leaves me now—it's a two-name situation—Bryan-Malcolm, Brandon-Malik, something like that, is sitting and staring at Kenny and me. He's a looker. A little young for my taste, but a looker. I found out BM is Preston's roommate. He's the uninvited plus-one of the plus-one. Preston is tacky like this. But so am I. I've definitely invited more than one person to functions when I was the plus-one.

"You don't have to," Kenny says. I feel some tension as he looks over at Brandon-Malik, Alberto, and Preston. "I'm going to go get a drink. Thanks for the dance."

Kenny unwraps his arms from around me.

"Thank you, Kenny, for the dance," I say. "And tell little Kenny to stop hitting my leg next time." I try to lighten the mood with a joke and head back to my table.

As I pass the beignet bar, I notice Elijah entering the ballroom. Butterflies. My stomach is filled with butterflies. I'm happily nervous he made it! Then I notice Savannah waddling over to the entrance. She doesn't know Elijah's face, so she's on it to see who's intruding on her party territory. Damn it, I gotta make it across the room to make it to him before she starts a long-winded and investigative conversation with him.

I make it to Elijah at the same time as Savannah, who asks with her *white* voice, "Heeyyyy, I'm Savannah, are you here with anyone?"

"Indeed he is!" I say, a little overconfident and excited. *Chill, Zaire. Be chill!* I hug Elijah.

"Pleasure to meet you, Savannah, I'm Elijah, I use they/them/theirs or he/him/his pronouns." He extends his hand to shake Vannah's hand. "You're Z's sister, right?"

"Indeed I am! You know about me?" Savannah says with a big smile and gives her hand to shake.

"Yes, he does," I say and hug Elijah. I'm surprised at this public display of affection in front of my sister and family. "I talk about all of the JamesGang to Elijah."

I do not know what overcomes me, but I kiss him. Kiss his soft juicy lips right in front of my sister. At my thirtieth party. Elijah is also caught off guard by my overt excitement, but kisses me back and laughs.

"It's nice to see you, too, Z."

"You're so pretty," Savannah says, sliding in between us to walk us to the JamesGang table at the head of the room. "I mean, do you like the word *pretty*? I know some guys are weird about that."

"Thanks for the compliment!" Elijah says. "And heck no, I don't mind. I'm pretty fluid anyway. Gender is overrated."

"Quiet as it's kept." Savannah laughs.

Wow, I'm surprised my sister is so warm to Elijah. She's just met him.

When we get back to the table, Savannah introduces Elijah to Harlem and Langston.

"Y'all, this beau is Elijah and they're Zaire's date," she says and opens and glides her right arm across the air like she's showcasing them. "Elijah, these are the siblings."

"Yo! Nice to meet you!" Harlem gets up from the table and gives the Black-handshake-hug to Elijah.

"Hi handsome!" Langston says. "You made it right on time. We are about to give the birthday toast. Well, I am! Harlem, get a glass of champagne for Elijah."

Langston gives Elijah a hug, smiles, tugs the top of her dress, and makes her way to the stage.

Langston

Moments before Zaire's date Elijah arrives, I'm having a moment of panic and our baby brother Harlem pulls me aside.

"What are you carrying tonight, Langston?" Harlem asks, sitting next to me at our table. He puts his arm around me.

"Nothing, I'm just enjoying tonight," I say. "What are you carrying?"

Harlem always knows when I'm thinking about something.

"I'm feeling really good. Buzzed. Happy to be here with everyone looking good. But you've been kinda quiet tonight, not awkwardly quiet, just a little quiet."

Perhaps I should tell him I'm actually thinking about moving to DC. Soon as I finally earn my cosmetology license, I want to move. On second thought, he's already drunk, he'd tell Savannah, and Savannah will talk to Zaire, and the party will turn into them convincing me to stay in L.A. and close to everyone because we are *all we got.*

So I lie and take the peacemaker Switzerland role I usually take in the JamesGang.

"I've been thinking about this toast I have to give in a minute," I say. "You know Vannah got me talking in front of all these people! You know I despise public speaking. Just because *she* feels fat with her pregnant belly. Heffa."

"I knew something was up. Don't do the toast."

Harlem is so blasé. Always is. I guess that's why everyone in the JamesGang likes him. I give him an eye roll.

"Don't...don't do it?"

"At some point you gotta start doing what you want to do and stop doing what you don't want to do," Harlem says. "Vannah asked me to do it because she said I'm closest and queerest to Zaire, but I told her no, she should do it because she's the next oldest to Zaire."

"You make it sound so easy, Harlem," I say, half believing my own words. "It's because you're the baby."

"It's not because I'm the *baby*," Harlem says and takes a sip of his drink. "Well, maybe it is, but it's mostly because I observe y'all. I learn what *not* to do by looking at y'all do what y'all really don't want to do."

Harlem's intoxicated behind is on a roll.

"Y'all. Who is the *y'all* you're referring to?" I ask.

"All y'all," he says. "But mostly you and Zaire. Both of y'all are people pleasers."

I do not have time to respond because Savannah interrupts us with an introduction of Zaire's date. Then she signals to me that it's time for the toast. Ready or not, here I go.

As I walk to the podium I hear Harlem in my head: *Stop doing what you don't want to do.* I am shaking, a mixture of nerves from public speaking and the thought of taking Harlem's advice about this speech and that I want to tell them I want to move to DC.

"Hi everyone, I'm Langston, Zaire's other sister."

I take a breath. I am really nervous. But I continue.

"I am supposed to read this speech that my sister wrote, celebrating our big brother," I go and look around the room. Everyone is looking at me. All eyes on me. All 126 people—because Savannah didn't want odd numbers messing up the seating at Zaire's party.

I continue.

"But that'll be just like me, doing something I do not want to do, just to please folks. I love my brother and I'm happy we are here celebrating Zaire. But I hate public speaking. What some of you do not know is that both my big brother and my big sister are always doing things behind the scenes for us, and maybe for some of you. Savannah will probably say that the party was planned by the three of us, but in reality, she planned it all. And she wrote this wonderful speech for the toast. So, since she wrote it, and since I am pretty much done with public speaking for the night, I'm going to take my little brother's advice," I pause and look directly at Harlem to mouth *thank you*, "and respectfully decline from reading it. Can you all help me welcome the woman behind this masquerade ball, my beautiful and understanding big sister, Savannah. Savannah James, please waddle to the podium and give this toast."

Zaire

Once again, the JamesGang shows up and shows out in grand style. I am happy. Elijah is happy. My family is happy. I do not know what happened to Kenny, as I didn't see him during my speech and thank you remarks. Nonetheless, I'm thirty. Fucking THIRTY, my God. Let the good times roll!

WINTER

ZAIRE

ICYF: Love Is Everywhere

It's Monday morning and the first day of winter. This morning I wake up thirty minutes before my alarm. I feel well rested, so I do not try to sleep longer. I have the person I've been dating—unofficially exclusively—for over a month on my mind. Elijah.

Elijah is perfect. Well, not perfect in the way that they can't do wrong. But perfect in the way they make me feel. I have never, I repeat, *never* met anyone who has made me feel like this.

Before meeting and dating Elijah, I wasn't aware of the fact that one of my love languages is affirmations. Elijah affirms, compliments, and encourages me all day long. They're so intentional about their words and actions. I don't even know what I am doing anymore. I honestly don't even think I deserve such wonder. I know I shouldn't think this way, because I am deserving of good things. I just, at times, question the universe, asking what have I done to deserve someone so great.

I've never dated anyone so centered in who they are, so clear about what they like and do not like. They rarely get upset but when they do, it's never for too long. It's as if they are fully present in knowing when and what to use energy on. I'm learning so much about myself through knowing Elijah. We are so good together. They are so good for me, so right, it must be wrong, somewhere, somehow.

I think I'm starting to push them away. I'm not intentionally doing it. It just happens. It's just happening. Whenever I'm too giddy about them, I force myself to calm down. I tell myself to be reserved, pretend to be cool, calm, and collected. Elijah notices when I'm trying to play cool, although they don't know that's what I'm doing. They ask what's on my mind, and I usually smirk and say, "Nothing, just you."

In the beginning, it was easier for me to allow myself to go with the flow. I didn't think much about how easy it was for me to like them. Elijah's so easy to like. So easy to love. And that's the thing, how can they be so easy to love? Here I am waiting for my divorce to be finalized and already finding myself falling in love. What the entire blue fuck.

I'm naturally inquisitive, which makes me an easy researcher at my job. Okay, fine, a Googler. At work, I spend much of my day reading diversity articles and creating presentations. Recently, I've started to use my work time reading articles pertaining to my personal life, like about finding new love and the process of divorces—both queer and straight.

After reading about other people's divorces, I'm confused. Many people in these articles say taking a year or two from dating helps them recenter and refocus. I barely took a couple months. Knowing this has really started to amplify my insecurities. In short, I don't want to hurt Elijah, like I think I did Kenny. What if he's a rebound? I've read all about rebounds. I can't hurt them. So for this week, I'm forcing distancing myself from Elijah. I made up five rules that I'm giving myself to follow.

1. Do not send my usual "good morning" call or text first.
2. Do not spend the night at their apartment or have them stay the night at my apt more than once this week. Or maybe not at all.
3. Do not accept more than one of their spontaneous invites to a random midweek lunch, or an underground art party; or it's-Wednesday-and-the-moon-is-nice special dinner at their apartment.

4. Do not respond to their texts right away; turn on text receipts.
5. Do not tell them you love them. Do not text them you love them. Do not love them.

❖

Tuesday: December 22

I arrive to work an hour before Jada. This is rare—she's the early one. The office is quiet. I've already read and replied to five emails, so I deserve a mini break that I'm taking right now. I walk to the window wall to watch the people walking outside. The air is brisk. L.A. winter clothes are my favorite, wardrobe for fashion and not weather. Think infinity scarves and short-sleeved shirts.

At 8 a.m., my Apple watch sends a reminder. I thought I'd removed this date from all of my e-calendars. Thanks to the damn iCloud, I am now forced to think about the day. Today, December 22, is my anniversary. My wedding anniversary. All of a sudden a wave of heat rushes through my body. I am flooded with memories of Mario and me. My heart starts to palpitate as I tell myself to breathe deep, slow breaths. I leave the window and walk to the restroom, hoping to rinse my face off and cool down.

"Good morning, Zaire, you're here early." Elena, the graduate student intern, greets me.

I continue to walk past her without saying a word.

When I make it to the single-stall all-gender restroom, I am half a second away from crying. I lock myself in. I just need a few moments to myself because today is my anniversary. Or would have been my anniversary. We really weren't a bad partnership. It was full of love. So much love for each other.

When we had "us" time, without all the people, without all of the extra facade of perfect for the family, for the friends and the fans, when it was just us, we were so good together for so long. We just got comfortable. He more than I got comfortable. He stopped noticing me, really seeing me. His listening skills started to dwindle; we'd talk and listen, but more times than not, he wouldn't hear me.

I still love Mario. But if these few months have taught me anything, it's this small but powerful fact—love sometimes just isn't enough.

After staring at myself in the mirror with tears cascading down my face, like I'm Janet Jackson in the movie *Poetic Justice*, I decide to get myself together. My phone vibrates and I do not check it. I turn on the water and let it run a bit so that it can heat up. I place my hands underneath the faucet, making a bowl shape. The water fills them up. I bow down over the sink, meeting my hands on the way up to my face. I wash away the tears. I wash away the sadness. I do this two more times, just to feel the warm water on my face, wishing to add another memory to this day.

"Hey, Z, you okay in there?" Jada whispers through the door.

I say nothing. Elena must have told Jada that I was in here. That heaux. Elena is quickly becoming one of my faves, so I'll forgive her this one time.

I pull out my phone and see there's a text from Elijah.

Morning Z for Zad, Zad for Zaddy, I start to giggle before I finish the text, *this was on my spirit this morning and thought to share with you. Whatever feelings today gifts you with, feel them.*

Why is Elijah this way? So damn easy to love.

I do not have the adequate words to share how I'm feeling, so I heart the message and reply, *Good morning E for...elephant?*

I hope he gets my humor.

Elijah "HAHAs" my text. He gets my humor. He gets me.

I walk to the door and open it. Jada is rested on the doorframe. Looking at me with puppy eyes.

"I'm okay," I say.

Jada hugs me and whispers, "Of course you are. Even if you are not."

❖

Wednesday, December 23

I'm working from home today. No one is really at the office today anyhow. I've decided to use the empty apartment to be with myself. Yesterday's near meltdown took me out!

Today, it is in my plan to seclude myself from the outside world for as long as I can. The phone and the MacBook are both set to my infamous Do Not Disturb. Times like these, I so appreciate the option to partially tap out from this high-tech world with the Do Not Disturb feature. It allows me to check in when I want to check in, versus receiving a notification and feeling like I automatically have to respond. Because that's who I am: I respond. I cannot actively ignore for too long.

I use three hours this morning to focus on myself before I attempt to do any work-work. I turn on some lo-fi hip-hop and stretch on my yoga mat. When that is done I go to the kitchen and see I do not have many groceries, so breakfast is a protein bar, the last of edamame pods, and a green kombucha. Elijah has rubbed off on me. After I eat this pitiful meal, I go to the window and look at Kenny's place. It's dark, no movement. He's not home, hasn't been there in a few days. I figure he's back home for the holidays. The block is kind of quiet this week, too. Many of my neighbors are transplants, so I assume they go back to where they come from around this time.

Then close to noon, I open my laptop to begin work. I'm only dedicating two hours for this. I turn over my phone to just check it. No missed calls and a shit-ton of text messages, mostly from the JamesGang. Two are from Elijah wishing me a good morning and wondering if we could FaceTime tonight. It's been two hours since the text, so I respond with a good morning—technically 11:45 a.m. is still morning. Then I "like" the second message about FaceTime. The other text is from one of the ones in my past hoetation—Max, saying *Hey, stranger*. I forgot I had given him my actual number off the app. I go to his name and block him. Nothing personal, he's sexually blessed. But the devil is a lie, I'm not trying to hoetate right now.

Savannah is the first to start off the texts this morning. They've been texting off and on for three hours.

Savannah: Good morning everyone!
Langston: Morning.
Harlem: Good morninnnnn beautiful people!
Savannah: I was thinking, maybe we shouldn't have a Christmas breakfast this year. Too early. How about we do a Christmas brunch or even dinner?
Harlem: I'm glad someone suggested it! 7 AM breakfast is played! Blessed be!
Langston: Sounds good to me. I say brunch, not dinner.
Savannah: Zaire, what do you think?

I check the timestamp to that question; it reads 9:34 a.m.

Savannah: So, you're ignoring us?
Harlem: "Precious!"
Langston: "Precious, you hear me talking to you!"

Savannah sends a gif of Mo'nique from the movie *Precious*. They all "HAHA" the gif.

I check the timestamp again. It reads 10:30 a.m.

Savannah: If you do not respond to these text by noon, I'm coming to find you.
Langston: Oh, Lordt

Harlem "likes" Savannah's text.

It is 11:56 a.m. when I respond. I "like" the brunch suggestion and text *Good morning! I had my phone on Do Not Disturb. I'm working from home, so have to stay focused.*

Then it hits me. Christmas is really less than two days away, and I haven't bought anyone anything. I open up another tab on my laptop and type in Amazon Prime.

❖

Thursday, December 24

"I hope you don't mind too much that I've popped up unannounced."

"Well, this is a surprise," Elijah says. "I can't lie, you've been a tad distant these few days. And I thought it was because it's the holidays. I imagine it could be tough during this time, without your parents, and your divor—"

I kiss Elijah before he finishes the sentence. I've followed all of my dumbass rules up until this very moment.

We sit in Elijah's living room around his coffee table, which is actually a stack of polished and painted recycled wooden pallets. Elijah's minimalist style is an interesting turn-on for me. There are scented candles burning at the altar in the corner of the room by the modern record player that's intentionally designed to look vintage.

I'm feeling insecure that I'm not following my rules by being here, so I run off a series of ridiculous questions, "Did you have plans tonight? Are you expecting someone? If you are that's totally cool, I mean, I know we aren't exclus—"

Elijah kisses me. I was bombarding him with too much too quick. Elijah is always telling me to slow down when I'm on a roll. He'd say, "Zai, slow down. Slow your brain."

"It's Christmas Eve, and the only plan I had was to go to my parents' home late tonight or early tomorrow morning."

Elijah walks to the wine cabinet and grabs a bottle and two glasses.

"I don't want to change your plan from going to your parents' tonight," I say trying to sound convincing.

"Zai, stop it. You aren't changing my plans. I hadn't decided if I was going to drive tonight or tomorrow morning."

"Well, you can still decide," I say. "I do not want to be a factor."

Well, maybe I do want to be a factor. It's been a few months, I can be a factor now, right?

"You're here now, Z, so you are a factor. That's fine with me. You're a factor. You *can* be factor."

Elijah says this and waits for a response. This conversation is getting serious real quick.

"Okay. I'm a factor on Christmas Eve!" I say with a giant grin and head nod. I open the bottle of cabernet and pour us both a glass.

"A toast to you being a factor *tonight*!" Elijah raises his glass. "An ex-factor." He laughs.

I clink my glass with his before he could say, "I'm just kidding." Elijah is funny and sexy.

We spend the next hour catching up on our week. Sharing stories about our favorite Christmas and holiday rituals. I share that for Christmas we do JamesGang gift exchange. We pull names around Thanksgiving time and each person is responsible to gift one gift to the name they pulled. I tell him Savannah and I usually gift everyone something smallish regardless of if we got their name or not. I also share that we try not to make Christmas a grand production anymore, not since Mama passed. Christmas was a grand day when Mama was alive. Instead of grand, we make it special, not grand. We can't, it's still too hard, even all these years later.

Elijah shares that his Filipino paternal granddad still dresses up as Santa Claus for Christmas dinner and calls everyone a "ho, ho, hoe" all night. He's never spoken about his Filipino ancestry nor his grandparents. But he's so happy sharing this story, so I do not ask about his Filipino side. That can be a conversation for another time.

After our second glass of wine, we are nestled in each other's beings. At some point in the evening Elijah put on the Fantasia *Christmas After Midnight* vinyl record. This album is grown and sexy Christmas, and it's really setting the mood. I kiss his forehead. Then his lips. Then his neck. He kisses my neck. Then he heads south.

"Can I kiss Zad?" Elijah asks.

"You sure can."

Elijah begins to unwrap his early Christmas present by unzipping my pants to get to what he calls Zad.

"Wait, right here?" I ask. "What if your housemate comes home?"

Elijah keeps kissing Zad. He looks up at me with Zad on his lips and says, "Transplant," then places Zad in his mouth. I am in ecstasy because it's been over a week since I've had a release. This feels so good, but I am having a hard time understanding what Elijah means by *transplant*.

"Oohhh…my Lord, this feels good," I say and moan. "But, wait. What do you mean, transplant?"

Elijah takes Zad out of his throat. He stands up, takes off his sweatpants and shirt, and is standing in front of me with a burgundy thong, and pretending that a mistletoe is between him and Zad.

"My roomie is a transplant. Cool thing about having a room-mate that's not from here, they leave during the holidays. They've been away since Monday and will not be back until after the new year."

Elijah gets back to the floor. "Now, take off your clothes."

❖

Friday, December 25

At 3 a.m. I wake up to my phone ringing. At this hour, the only ones that can get through to my line are my siblings. My phone is automatically set on Do Not Disturb every night. Elijah and I have fallen asleep in the living room. I slide his head off my chest to grab the phone. This wakes him up.

"Hello," I say, clearing my throat.

"Savannah's having the baby!" It's my brother Harlem.

"What?" I say, getting up off the floor. Elijah wipes his eyes and sits up, too.

"Savannah is in labor. I'm on my way to the hospital. Meet us there."

I turn on the living room light to put on my pants. Time is moving fast and my mind is all over the place. Savannah is having the baby a month before her delivery date. This can't be a good thing. Elijah is putting on clothes as well. He's coming? Elijah notices me pacing and struggling to find my keys that are actually in my jogger pockets.

"Zai, you want to take a moment before we drive?" Elijah says, walking to the kitchen.

"No, I'm good, just need to find my keys. She's actually having the baby, I gotta hurry up!"

Elijah walks back to the living room with two cups of water and hands me one.

"Here, have some water."

I take the water and gulp it.

"Thank you, Elijah. You sure you want to go with me? I do not know how long babies or deliveries take."

Elijah stares at me. He isn't looking at me with suspicion. He's truly processing, taking into account if joining me is a good decision. I love that about him. He's mindful of what works for him and what doesn't. He's very balanced this way.

"Yes, I'm sure. This is big, I want to be there." He says this with a sure calmness that disappears when he adds, "Savannah is giving birth!"

Without further hesitation I say, "Okay, let's go!"

Elijah opens the jacket closet and grabs a black sweatshirt, then passes a jean jacket to me. He walks over to the altar and pulls a piece of sage out of the bundle, lights a match, and burns the sage. He smudges the altar, himself, then walks to me and swirls the burning sage around my feet then up to my head, giving me a halo. He lets the sage piece finish burning and says, "Now we are ready," then kisses my forehead. All of this grounds me; my heart stopped beating so fast and my palms have dried. I am now calm and warm.

❖

Elijah and I are the last to make it to the delivery party. When we enter the room, I stand at the doorway and look at my family. Langston and Harlem are standing on the right side of the hospital bed. Anthony is lying next to Savannah in the hospital bed. There's a little baby in Savannah's arms. Anthony's parents are sitting down on the left side of the bed holding each other. I start to cry and Elijah is holding on to my arm. Love is all over this room.

"Come meet your nibbling," Anthony says.

I make it to the bed with tears falling.

"Zaire, meet Zai Noel James-Martin. Zai Noel James-Martin, meet Uncle Zaire," Savannah says with tears gracefully flowing down her face.

The best Christmas present. What a beautiful and grand Christmas.

KENNY

ICYF: Get It Out, Whatever It Is

I really didn't want to do this, but my therapist thought I should, I want to say. But I delete it.

Hey, I text instead.

I put my phone down and walk to the front picture window. I'm looking into Zaire's window, but it's dark and no one apparently is home. Texting Zaire would be much easier, now that I've gone to his birthday party a couple months ago and we're somewhat on speaking terms.

But this text is to Brandon-Malik.

I saw him at Zaire's birthday party back in November—which I don't know why he was invited—but I did a Mariah Carey "I don't know her" moment and ignored Brandon-Malik most of that night. Silly, because I really did want to talk to him, given I'd never responded to his Drake text or his *hi* text months before that.

Playing reindeer games. Not what someone on the cusp of forty and in therapy should be doing.

A quick Christmas Eve FaceTime session with Thea the therapist last week, and I knew I was above and beyond playing games with Brandon-Malik or any other person in my life.

The phone chimes. I take my time going back across the room to get it.

Hey, Brandon-Malik texts back.

So this is how it's gonna be. Hmmm. I start to type, so he can see my bubbles letting him know I'm replying. Then I delete and pause, so the bubbles disappear, letting him know I'm not replying. I repeat, type, delete, type, delete. He's on my time. Now.

Reindeer games. Just a little bit of petty.

I had you on my mind, he texts.

Shit. What am I to say to that? I am on a mission. Stay focused, Kenny.

I have some things on my mind and I'd like to share them with you, I say.

Brandon-Malik FaceTimes.

I stare at the phone and panic.

I decline it.

Hey, did you decline me? Brandon-Malik texts quickly.

Yeah, I declined. Let's meet instead.

When?

In an hour. The park.

What park?

THE park.

THE park is the park where I used to run and see Brandon-Malik play basketball before I'd eventually see him at the gym, and before him sending me notes in my DMs. He should know what I mean by *the park*. If he doesn't, then he doesn't really know me and definitely didn't know us.

Oh THAT park. Bet. See you there.

One hour.

Brandon-Malik hearts the *one hour*. I thumbs-up his *oh THAT park* message.

❖

I circle the block three times. I'm nervous. And probably looking like a stalker, perv, up-to-no-good creeper to anyone in the neighborhood who might have their eye on me and my car.

I used to avoid things that were emotionally hard. Now I'm facing them. So glad my work with Thea the therapist is paying off, though I know it's a long-term process. I wish I'd had this courage through the year and half Brandon-Malik and I were together. Together should be in quotes. Were we really ever together? If we were really together, would we have had the break-up-to-make-up-to-break-up-to-make-up action? If we were really together, would we get together, go out on dates, and do anything together only when I took the initiative? If we were really together, would he only initiate our hanging out only when he wanted something—money, head, a cheerleader/coach/therapist, a quickie?

Wish I'd had the courage to ask those questions *when* those things were happening. Wish I'd had the courage to ask about that one guy liking all of his pics (yeah, I noticed), that same one guy whose pics he's always liking (definitely noticed that), his "no labels, no commitments, no rules" rule (which hurt, but I accepted it because I thought it was the best way to keep him in my life), his questionable employment (Mama's rule, in case you forgot), the pics I found floating on gay Twitter last Christmas of him and his ex with #RelationshipGoals as the hashtag (I could've died, but didn't die, but never said anything), his ex popping up mysteriously during our dates after watching Brandon-Malik's or my social media storylines (stalker), the times he'd go ghost on me during our relationship (quite frequently), only to call me up when he apparently was done with the ex or wanted something from me (more than I care to remember).

Wish I hadn't stuck by him when he was broke. Wish I hadn't tried to get him legit jobs, so that he didn't have to do his OnlyFans shit online. Wish I hadn't been his summer in the wintertime. Wish I hadn't spent so much time wondering if I was good enough or not good enough for a man whose only claim to fame is a few thousand followers on Instagram and who ain't doing shit with their lives. Wish I hadn't lost myself or forgotten who I was.

But it's a new day and I'm initiating the conversation with Brandon-Malik, on my time and in my own way. Finally.

On my fourth circle around the park, I notice Brandon-Malik approaching a bench adjacent to the basketball courts. He's on time. Wearing gray joggers, a denim jacket, black T-shirt, and headphones that look like the ones I bought him over the winter holidays a year earlier. I pull into a spot near the courts. He notices me right away and walks my way, his gray joggers showing off the best of what I remember…and forgot, down there. He greets me when I get out the car.

"Hey."

"Hey."

"Happy New Year," he says. "It's been a minute."

"Happy New Year."

"If I'd known we were gonna meet up today, I'da brought your Christmas present."

"You mean bought?" I ask and almost smile, but jokes with Brandon-Malik are not on the agenda.

"Okay, you right, you right," he says. Throws a fist bump my way. "Money a little tight now. People ain't got time or spare coins for sessions during the holidays, you know? I started driving Lyft till…"

"I didn't come expecting a gift, Brandon-Malik."

We stare at each other. I'm enamored, once again, with his beautiful pretty-boy looks. It's too bad he just doesn't have the smarts or initiative to go with his beautiful Black man magic. A million Brandon-Malik and Kenny memories start to flood my mind. At this time, they're mostly good. But I don't want to get caught up in the rapture of a love gone by, so I focus before I lose control and head back into the world of Brandon-Malik.

"You look and smell like good credit and grown-up decisions, Kenny," he says and looks me up and down and then in the eye. "Damn."

"Let's walk."

I set the car alarm and point in the direction of a cement path going through the center of the park.

"Whatever you want, Kenny," he says and pulls the headphones down off his ears and places them around his neck. "It's good to see you. You look good."

I will not say anything back about his looks—my weakness, so I go, "Thanks."

"You ignored me at that party," he says. He's talking about Zaire's party. He doesn't know who Zaire is, so he has to say *that* party. "That was our first time seeing each other in six months. I felt attacked. I was hurt."

"You were hurt? Really."

"Yeah. But that's probably nothing compared to what I've done to you."

"What have you done?"

"Nothing," he says. "Not enough. But I thought the way you ignored me at that party was doing the most."

I'm not about to let him get ahead of this conversation, but it's exactly what he's doing. Or trying to do.

"It was a busy night. I didn't really want to be there."

"Do you want to be here?" Brandon-Malik asks. Nervous smile. "With me, now?"

Ugh.

"Didn't I tell you to be here?" I'm being too harsh. "So, yes, I do want to be here, with you, now."

"Wow. You're still cute when you're pressed."

Brandon-Malik puts an arm around my shoulder and pulls me near him. I cannot tell if the rush in my stomach are butterflies or anxiety, but I will not melt or swoon. I pull away.

"Brandon-Malik, I'm not here to pretend."

"Pretend?"

"Like this is just another get-back-together scene for us," I say. "This isn't."

"I didn't say it was," he says and smiles. That smile. "I miss you, though. I thought Preston told you how much I missed you when y'all went out to Palm Springs without me."

"Preston did," I say. I wonder how much Brandon-Malik knows about the episode with his roommate, but now is not the time to figure that out. "I was a mess on that trip and I guess I didn't believe him. Or didn't want to believe him. At that time, you'd made no direct effort other than a 'hi' text."

"But that's okay," he says. "We're here now. And now you know. How I felt...and feel."

Let me cut straight to the point. No reindeer games.

"Did you miss me when you said you couldn't be there for me on the day of my mother's funeral last summer?"

"BALL!" someone yells when a random basketball hits Brandon-Malik's side. He picks the ball up and holds it for a second before he throws it back to the players on the court.

Brandon-Malik is still quiet. He's not ready for that question, apparently, and I do not want to let him off the hook.

"Cat got your tongue?" I say, looking directly into his dark eyes. I am quite amazed at myself. But really, I do not feel angry. Just. Focused.

"I do not know what to say," he says with a bowed head.

"You know, when you texted me, TEXTED me that four-page letter, I…" I say and find myself getting emotional, feeling as if I'm about to relive that week, so I take a breath. "I didn't know what to do about you. I had other things to do. I had to call the family, then the church, then I had to organize obituary pictures. I had to figure out songs, my mom's outfits, insurance policies and funeral home payments. And then at night, when I thought I would have someone to just be there, when I thought as much as I'd been there for you, even when you took me for granted, I wanted someone—*you*—to be there. Just to listen. Just to ask what's up. I didn't need much. I do *not* need much. As much as I gave you—"

"Kenny, I—" Brandon-Malik attempts to interrupt.

"I'm not done, Brandon-Malik."

"Go on, then," he says and leans against a short brick wall lining the edge of the park and sidewalk. I sit next to him and just talk into the air.

"I let all the other things go…the lies, ghosting, your rules about no commitments and no labels, your pics popping up online…But when you said you couldn't be there for me…I felt like you punched me in the gut…Like I was just some stranger on the street to you… But yet, you found time to be out in the streets almost every day— snapping pics with new guys and your ex, going on beach outings, attending pool parties in downtown L.A., driving to Palm Springs—

while I was with my family taking care of funeral arrangements. You wanna talk about hurt? That hurt."

"I was scared, Kenny."

"Scared like when you accepted a thousand dollars from my mom during my graduation party week?"

He turns my way, mouth open, shook and shocked that I found out that piece of information.

"I...I..." he stutters and puts his hands up like he's caught. Looks away again.

"And then you text me a random *hi* this summer after ending things...and what's up with you texting me out of the blue a few weeks ago at three in the morning about a Drake concert being your favorite date with me, as if nothing...After all this time, when I've thought about you, wondered if I did something to make you not want to be in my life and not want to support me, when I've doubted my own sanity for wanting you in my life..."

"That text was my way of saying I missed you all these months."

"And you know the thing that's been eating at me for these few months? All of the things that have happened, I've allowed them to happen. But I'm not mad at you anymore."

"Thanks," he says and exhales a sigh of relief. "You're not?"

"No," I say. "Because once I realized that I've played along for all of these months, I had to put to rest the anger that I had toward you, Brandon-Malik, and give some to me. I had to allow myself to be angry at myself. And to mourn...you, my mother, my job, everything I thought was certain and real in my life. And I did. I *really* did. And now I'm not angry. I do become sad because I think about what a fool I've been for and about you, but I'm not angry. Therapy helps, you know."

"Thank you," he says. "I don't know what to say."

I turn to him. Put my hand over his hand on his right thigh.

"You don't have to say anything."

"You deserve better, Kenny," he says. "I always had you up on this pedestal because of your accomplishments, how you've got your life together, you're Black, smart, woke. I thought I could give up my superficial life of nothing for someone with everything I want to be. You deserved better. You deserve better, Doc."

"I appreciate that, Brandon-Malik," I say. "It still hurts hearing that, though, because all along you could have done better. I could have demanded better. I will...now."

He looks back at me, finally, in the eyes. "I love you."

"Don't say what you don't mean."

"I love you, Kenny, I really do," he says. "I know I've been terrible at showing you. And you're the best person I've ever hung out with."

"Hung out with," I say. "You can't even say *dated*. Not that I need you to say that. It would have mattered to me at the time."

"Kenny, I'm sorry. Really, I'm sorry."

"I know," I say and lean over to hug Brandon-Malik. He hugs back. "In case you forgot what you've given up in me. I pray the same thing you've done to me never happens to you."

SPRING

Kenny

ICYF: Break the Pattern

"And look at me, Thea," I say. "All that and I have not fallen apart."

I'm sitting in Thea the therapist's office right after St. Patrick's Day. We're well past the ninety-day breakup plan and well into grief counseling and homework. Our work together is getting more focused and will be winding down soon for a number of reasons—one, I'm getting back to me; and two, my mom's life insurance money and my vacation money payout from the university is running out. So I gotta be well-intentioned about our visits, because they cost.

And I will definitely have to get a job soon. Even with some speaking gigs rolling in, Thea the therapist points out that my life could mirror that of Brandon-Malik—Black, jobless, aimless, cute and credentialed (in an academic way, not the online way)—if I don't focus on the next chapter of my life and the visions I've shared with her about community university, helping Black people, justice, etc...

Thea's got a chart up in her office, a visual reminder of the progress I've made in the months working with her. She's got crossmarks through Zaire's, Alberto's, Preston's, and Brandon-Malik's names, hearts next to Cecily's and Tonya's names, a question mark next to Carlos's name, and a tree-like symbol next to my mom's name. Seeing the chart, and the timeline of my therapy, helps me to feel a sense of accomplishment and a sense of possibilities. I've stopped calling myself a mess and I actually don't feel like my life is a mess anymore.

"I'm proud of you and your work, Kenny," Thea the therapist says. "What else is left?"

"Mmmmmm." I fold my arms.

"What about that question mark next to your best friend's name?"

"Mmmmmm."

"Fifteen-plus years of friendship," she says. "I can't tell you what to do. I can only point out a pattern, and it's up to you to do the work. Avoiding Carlos is part of your pattern."

I know Thea the therapist is right. It's been five months since Carlos and I have talked, texted, messaged, or group chatted. Tyra and Lily are super careful not to mention Carlos's name when we chat, and I'm sure they do the same when they're chatting with Carlos. In a little over a month, it'll be commencement time, and just like the doctoral class that finished a year before us, it'll be our turn to help hood the new group of educational leaders and doctors. So I'll have to see Carlos. Eventually.

"Damn, Thea," I say. "It's almost been a year since my mom and sisters were out here for my graduation. That just hit me when you mentioned Carlos."

"What are you carrying, Kenny?"

I've loved that phrase, that question, ever since I started therapy with Thea.

"Life goes by fast," I say. "And we only get one…that we know of."

"So what you gone do?"

I look around Thea's office, notice the stones, the sage, the sayings taped along the walls and furniture. Everywhere but her eyes.

"Okay," is all I can say at the moment.

Zaire

ICYF: K.T.S.E.

The apartment is quiet. My divorce has been finalized. I thought I would be overjoyed that I am legally single again. I thought perhaps I'd want to send a text to JamesGang saying "drinks on me, I'm legally single in these streets!" But those feelings are not here. For the past couple of days all I've thought about is Mario's dad, Maurice, aka Pops, and my niece, Marie. Ex-niece now, I guess. She'll be ten in a few days, and I haven't seen or spoken to my ex-family in almost a year. I wonder how they are doing, if they think of me as often as I think of them. I wonder if Marie is still practicing the guitar, or if Pops finally stopped smoking like he said he would all the years Mario and I were together.

"You want some plantains? I'm about to put some in the oven," Alberto says, walking to the kitchen.

I didn't hear him enter the living room. I was off staring out the window, deep in thought, mesmerized by the row of birds-of-paradise aligning both Kenny's place and my place. They are my favorite flowers and are still my calming place. Many of them managed to stay alive during the winter, but now that it's spring, all of them are vibrant green, yellow, and orange.

I've always had a special connection to birds-of-paradise.

The spray on my dad's casket was made mostly of birds-of-paradise. I was too young to be a pallbearer, so I just sat right in front of the casket admiring the flowers. I remember wanting to jump into the casket with my dad, never wanting to get out. I had lost my dad—my best friend—to a traumatic police shooting experience. At that age, I didn't have the language to describe all of the emotions I was going through. I thought I was going to die—that pain, that loss, made me feel like I was going to die. For months after my father's death, the sight of birds-of-paradise haunted me. Seeing them would take me back to the funeral, then the murder, then thoughts of police harming my family's development forever, then a forlorn air would linger for the whole day or days. It wasn't until intense therapy that I was able to process the feelings and thoughts associated with the flowers. I went from believing I was going to die from indescribable hurt, to surviving the pain. What the therapist helped me do was feel my grief and, most importantly, recategorize the sight of birds-of-paradise.

Now, they no longer symbolize pain, death, and hurt. When I stare at birds-of-paradise, they reaffirm that I can get through a lot. I can survive, and with a little help from people who love me, and perhaps a therapist, I can even thrive.

"*Oye, nene, quieres o no?*" Alberto says from the oven where he's standing.

"Yes, I'll eat a few," I respond and open my laptop.

"What you got planned this afternoon?"

"Thriving," I say.

"*Eso!* K.T.S.E!" Alberto sings. "Keep That Same Energy, because that sounds like a good plan."

I decide to finally take Kenny's and my siblings' advice and revisit therapy. I open the saved tabs on my laptop, which lead me to the local QTPOC therapists. I select four of the therapists, copy down their emails, open my email, and BCC them all.

Greetings,

I'm a 30-year-old, queer Black man living in West Hollywood. This week my divorce finalized and I think I have all of the makings of screwing up the healthiest relationship I think I've ever had. I'm seeking a therapist who specialize in grief, trauma, and marriage and family therapy. My work schedule is pretty laxed, but I think

Saturday morning sessions would do me well. I have some experience with therapy and I think I need to bring back the practice of consciously focusing on my mental health and self-care. Based on your website you seem to accept my PPO insurance. If that information isn't correct, do you offer other payment options?

Today, I'm trying to thrive. Emailing you is a big part of my thriving. I look forward to hearing back from you.

Best,
Zaire James

KENNY

ICYF: Let Go of Ego

"Thanks for not acting weird at commencement, Carlos," I say as we meet up on the sidewalk outside my condo. We're still in our red doctoral regalia. "I know I've been a jerk."

"The separate Lyfts was a jerk move on your part," Carlos says and rolls his eyes. We laugh. "But I'm glad Tyra and Lily made us talk. Or start to talk, anyway."

I'm glad, too, I think. It was time...and it was me and ego.

"Let's get outta this Harry Potter gear," I say and we make our way through the front gate, a quick stop at the mailbox, and up the stairs to my condo. "I'll order something on Postmates or Uber Eats."

"Food's cool," Carlos says. "Drinks are better."

"I gotcha covered."

"I'm glad we're talking again."

"Blame it on me," I say. "I can be stubborn sometimes. And rightly so."

"Real friends don't have to apologize or explain."

"Exactly," I say. "Missed you. Love you, Carlos."

As we enter my place, I remember that I'd forgotten to mention something else to Carlos in the midst of our we're-talking-again reunion. It's been that long.

"What's up with all the boxes, Kenny?"

"I never got to tell you until now," I say and put my house key on the corner of the kitchen bar. "I'm putting the condo up for sale.

I'm moving. You and Ricky in the market for another place to add to your empire?"

"Empire? Please," Carlos says. "Where're you moving to? Back to Monterey Park?"

We've got a lot to catch up on, obviously.

"You want dark, light, or wine?" I unzip and remove my regalia and set it on a barstool. A thousand-dollar robe Carlos and I'll wear just once a year, if that. Beautiful gowns, though.

"Let's keep it light today…vodka," Carlos goes. He's unzipping his regalia. "I've got commencement rehearsals all day tomorrow at CUELA. Can I get a hanger for this?"

"Ugh, CUELA, and yes, you know where they are," I go. "And please don't try and offer me any other jobs."

"I'm not."

I take two mango Ciroc and tonics into the living room and set them on top of a stack of U-Haul boxes I haven't filled up yet but am using as a stand-in for the coffee table, which I've already wrapped in plastic and placed in a Pod cubicle out back. Carlos returns from my bedroom, grabs a drink, sits on the end of the sofa nearest the picture window, and looks across the street at Zaire's window.

"What's up with the dynamic duo across the street?"

"Nothing," I say. "Cheers."

We clink glasses.

"Cheers," he goes. "Really? Nothing?"

I'm trying to remember how much I had a chance to share with Carlos about Zaire before I stopped talking to both of them. It's all a fog and now it's not important.

"Yep. Nothing. I went to Zaire's thirtieth party in November. We text and talk now and then, but nothing really."

"What about Brandon-Malik?"

"That's done," I say and take a long sip. "Done-done. Like this drink, done. I guess I'm parched. I haven't been drinking much lately."

"To be honest, I haven't drank much either," Carlos says. "Missed my drinking buddy—you! And this job with all they're tossing on my plate…I can't afford to go in tired, recovering, coming up or down from a buzz. They don't play when they add that management personnel label to your title."

"Fuck that shit," I go and then go back to the kitchen to make just one more drink for myself. I've got more packing to do this evening or in the morning. Trying to stay on schedule for the move. "I'm not going back to that enslaved-by-white-liberals campus life anymore."

"How's business?"

"It sucks," I say and return to the living room. "And I need a job."

"If you want…"

"Don't offer," I go. "Thanks, though. If I'm going back to a nine-to-five, it's going to be with Black people, Black students, and a Black community. I'm not giving up my talents, gifts, and doctoral-degree skills for other people's communities anymore."

"Cheers to that," Carlos says. "I kinda been thinking about the same thing, believe it or not. Tired of white administrators and white Latinx folks—yeah, I know I'm a white Mexican, too—upholding white supremacist policies and practices at CUELA. But I can't keep up with two mortgages and try to step out on my own."

"That's what having a husband is for. What does Ricky have to say? Do you talk to him about your dreams?"

"Ricky's open relationed himself to someone else," Carlos says. "He moved out before the new year."

"Men are trash," I say. Then decide I have to inject a little Thea the therapist into the conversation. "Men are not trash. It's what we allow that allows them to become trash."

"I'll drink to that," Carlos says. "And I'm not drinking any more. This is my first and last for the day."

"I feel bad that we let all these months go by without talking. That's my fault. I take responsibility."

"So many days I wanted to talk. Thank God I have my mom to…damn, I'm sorry."

"It's cool, Carlos," I go. "My mom is dead. Yours isn't. I'm glad you had and have her."

"I'm glad I have you, Kenny." We bump fists. "You're my best friend. I'm glad we're talking again."

"I'm glad we're talking again, too," I say. "Are you and Ricky done? For good?"

"I don't want to be done, but I think it's been on his mind for a while for whatever reason," he says. "If I'd known he was out, I never would have agreed to purchase the Palm Springs place. Divorce, if we go there, is messy and expensive."

"Thanks to the higher power I'm not married," I say. I think I'm buzzed, but I'm still in my full mind. "Selling this place will be easy. Lotta folks wanna move to West Hollywood. I'm out."

"Wow, less than a year in this place. Where are you moving to? Baldwin Hills? Ladera Heights? To be around more Black people?"

"No," I say. "Back to Ohio. To be around people I've almost forgotten but who have never forgotten about me."

"What? No…"

"Yeah. Ohio."

"But we're talking again. You can't leave."

"I know, right?" I say. "I can't believe it either. I'm out after WeHo Pride."

"So much has happened between the two of us," Carlos says, holding my shoulder. "Let's not go this many months ever again without talking."

I reach for Carlos's hand and we lock fingers.

"Also, Kenny, earlier I said real friends don't need to apologize," Carlos says, "That's not true. They do. I'm sorry for not reaching back out. I knew you were or are still grieving. Real friends know when to take space and come back."

"Real friends know. And for that I am sorry, too."

SUMMER

KENNY

ICYF: Move On

It's a little after seven in the morning, I just got out the shower, and I've got a few moments before the moving truck picks up the Pod container behind my building. I can't believe this is my last day in L.A. and West Hollywood. I sit on a box that gives me a perfect view of Zaire's window across the street, and pull out my journal.

> *This is where and how my West Hollywood story began and how it ends. In the picture window, a day after the Pride Festival, and the season of people moving in and out the neighborhood in early summer. This time, it's me who's moving out. I'm happy.*
>
> *Zaire threw a Pride gathering at his place yesterday, but it also doubled as a going-away party for me. That was nice of him. He's sweet. I sometimes wish we'd worked things out, but I'm also glad we worked out as friends. And no weird vibes either, even with Carlos, Ricky, Preston, Alberto, and even Brandon-Malik in the house. Cocktails helped. A clear point of view, focus, and the process of becoming helped more.*
>
> *It's funny how as soon as I set up a boundary with Brandon-Malik, and made it known we were not getting back together, he started trying to act right. Isn't that a cliché? They always want what they can't and won't*

have anymore. Started calling, texting, messaging, and eventually stopping by on occasion when he was in or near West Hollywood to hang out with Preston...just to say hello. He even introduced me to some of his popular Instagram friends, whenever we'd run into each other at one of the bars or clubs on Santa Monica. Always with a "Kenny is the best person I ever dated...and I let him get away...a doctor!" caveat to the conversation. I guess to show them what he was capable of snagging, the same way I used to brag to my crew about snagging a young, Black, popular social media "influencer" who really wasn't into me. Oh well, no more fairy tales, as Anita Baker once sang in a song called "Fairy Tales."

Reality. I'm looking forward to living near my family and giving back to the community that gave so much to me when I was growing up. They never forgot about me, something I appreciate, and now it's my turn. I don't know what life will bring as an adult, conscious Black and Queer man in Toledo, Ohio, but I'm up for the challenge. And if it doesn't work out in Toledo, Ohio...well, there are forty-nine other states...and the world! The best thing I realize now...that I'll never forget—I've got options!

The price I'm getting for selling this place will set me up for a few months to figure out what's next, given the much-lower cost of living in the Midwest. #BallerInOhio

The one thing I wish is I could find therapists like Naija and Thea bac—

A knock at the door interrupts my writing. Must have missed something from the movers, but I yell, "Come in. It's open."

It's Zaire. With a coffee carrier, a small brown bag, and a potted baby bird-of-paradise flower.

"You're an angel, Zaire," I say and help him with the coffee and the front door. "It's so early...after all the Pride drinking yesterday."

"I couldn't let you leave WeHo without saying goodbye... again."

We set the coffee carrier and flower on the counter and Zaire pulls me into his arms.

"You give the best hugs," I say and hug Zaire back, like we did last night before going our separate ways—Zaire, barhopping on Santa Monica; me, finishing up my packing. "Elijah's so lucky to have you."

"I know." Zaire pulls away. "I'm gonna miss you, neighbor."

Zaire stares at me and I can see in his basketball shorts that he'd be down for a morning quickie, but that's not gonna happen. Boundaries. People love trying to cross them. But had this been months ago... Anyway, I need to hit the road before L.A. traffic gets too crazy.

"I'm gonna miss you, too." I open the bag. "What do we have here?"

"I know you're back on your vegan tip," Zaire says. "So a couple vegan, gluten free, cardboard breakfast sandwiches."

"Blah, you and your jokes."

"The coffee with almond milk and a hint of that natural sweetener you like. Almond milk is vegan, yeah?"

I take a sip. It's good. I won't die if almond milk isn't vegan.

"I appreciate how you know me so well, Zaire. Thank you."

"I wish you weren't moving, Kenny," Zaire says. "But I understand."

"Thanks for understanding."

"I guess I'm taking your place as the BlaQueer elder around here."

"How about a yelder," I say. "That's a young elder. Ha ha. Corny joke time. And thirty ain't old. Not by a long shot."

"Ha," Zaire says and makes a face. "You're everything I hope to be when I turn forty. Which, by the way, you've never told anyone when your birth date is in May, so no one was able to give you a party. You suck. And you're weird."

"You're weird."

"No, you're weird, Kenny."

"No, you are, Zaire."

We laugh, smile, and stare. No kiss.

"So anyway," Zaire says and walks over to the picture window. "You're all set? For the cross-country drive?"

"Yeah," I say. "And that reminds me…"

I check my phone again to make sure I've got enough podcast favorites downloaded—*The Read, Jade & XD, Gettin' Grown, Daytime Confidential, The Friend Zone, Strange Fruit, Dem Black Mamas, Heat Rocks*, and *HIM*—to get me through the four- or five-day road trip to Ohio. Maybe six. I'm in no rush. What the old folks used to say—nothing to do, and all day to do it.

The phone rings while I'm getting my podcasts together. Must be the movers. I answer and put it on speaker.

"Kenny Kane? This is Jabari from the moving company."

"Yeah."

"We're exiting Santa Monica Boulevard right now. We'll be there to pick up your Pod and other items in, say…fifteen minutes."

"I'm ready. See you soon."

Zaire pouts his lips and looks like he's about to cry.

"I guess this is goodbye, huh?" He walks my way and hugs me.

"It's a 'see you later.'"

"If that's what you call it," Zaire says and leans in. This time, plants a kiss on my forehead. "Love you."

"Love you, too, Zaire."

My phone rings again. Probably the movers again. I answer and put on speaker again. Zaire sits at the kitchen bar, takes out his breakfast sandwich, sips on coffee.

"Kenny Kane?"

"Yeah. Are you all lost?"

"Sorry?"

"Oh, pardon me. Who's this? I thought you were my moving company."

"Sorry for the inconvenience. I hope to keep this brief, Kenny Kane. I'm Harper and we met at one of your presentations earlier this year."

I'm trying to remember all the contacts in my mind and phone, while also thinking about the movers who are on their way.

"Harper from DC? Yeah, I remember. Kinda."

"Awesome. Well, I never forgot your keynote at Brother Connection. And your story of resilience and persistence while completing your doctoral studies, losing your mother, navigating mental health, self-care, and wellness, and doing social justice work with marginalized students. It was riveting. You're unforgettable, Kenny Kane."

Zaire mouths *unforgettable* across the room at me. He also winks and sends a thumbs-up. We both smile.

"Thank you," I say, both to Harper and to Zaire.

"So I am chief of staff of a new team based in Chicago and DC, and I was talking about you, your talk, the work you do, and your story at our team meeting yesterday afternoon," Harper says. "Everyone was excited and glued to their seats listening to me talk about you. Thank goodness I had some video to share of your Brother Connection keynote."

"Wow, thanks," I say. "I'm flattered."

"We might have a place for you," Harper says. "It's open, either Chicago or DC, whatever you think might work best—that's if you're interested in a new opportunity. We think it fits with your vision of university in the community and helping marginalized people become their best selves. Your vision matches our organization's vision perfectly, to be honest. So we want to do a phone conference with you first, and if that works out—and I have no doubt about that working out—then an in-person and a thorough background check are next steps."

I'm shocked that this random guy at one of my random speeches or workshops remembers me. Then, again, I remember his words...I'm unforgettable.

"Refresh my memory, I seem to have forgotten," I say. "What's your team or organization again?"

Zaire sends me a silent high five across the room and starts twerking in front of the window to mess up my composure on this call. He stops immediately when we both hear what Harper has to say next.

"Hold on a second, Kenny," Harper says. "I'm connecting you now to Mrs. Obama."

In Case You Forgot,
give yourself another
chance.

About the Authors

Originally from Detroit, Michigan, **FREDERICK SMITH** is a graduate of the Missouri School of Journalism, Loyola University Chicago, and Loyola Marymount University. He lives in Los Angeles. He is author of *Play It Forward*, *Right Side of the Wrong Bed*, and *Down For Whatever*. Visit his website at www.FrederickLSmith.com.

CHAZ LAMAR was raised in the deserts and cities of Southern California by his Louisianan maternal grandparents. He is a graduate of Cal State LA and the University of San Francisco. Chaz's work as a poet, creative, writer is informed by his interest in sharing truth and stories, and exploring identity as an ever evolving, Black, queer, lovechild, Sagittarius. Visit his website at www.chazlamar.com.

Books Available From Bold Strokes Books

Accidental Prophet by Bud Gundy. Days after his grandmother dies, Drew Morten learns his true identity and finds himself racing against time to save civilization from the apocalypse. (978-1-63555-452-6)

In Case You Forgot by Fredrick Smith and Chaz Lamar. Zaire and Kenny, two newly single, Black, queer, and socially aware men, start again—in love, career, and life—in the West Hollywood neighborhood of LA. (978-1-63555-493-9)

Counting for Thunder by Phillip Irwin Cooper. A struggling actor returns to the Deep South to manage a family crisis but finds love and ultimately his own voice as his mother is regaining hers for possibly the last time. (978-1-63555-450-2)

Survivor's Guilt and Other Stories by Greg Herren. Award-winning author Greg Herren's short stories are finally pulled together into a single collection, including the Macavity Award–nominated title story and the first-ever Chanse MacLeod short story. (978-1-63555-413-7)

Saints + Sinners Anthology 2019, edited by Tracy Cunningham and Paul Willis. An anthology of short fiction featuring the finalist selections from the 2019 Saints + Sinners Literary Festival. (978-1-63555-447-2)

The Shape of the Earth by Gary Garth McCann. After appearing in *Best Gay Love Stories*, *HarringtonGMFQ*, *Q Review*, and *Off the Rocks*, Lenny and his partner Dave return in a hotbed of manhood and jealousy. (978-1-63555-391-8)

Exit Plans for Teenage Freaks by 'Nathan Burgoine. Cole always has a plan—especially for escaping his small-town reputation as "that kid who was kidnapped when he was four"—but when he teleports to a museum, it's time to face facts: it's possible he's a total freak after all. (978-1-163555-098-6)

Death Checks In by David S. Pederson. Despite Heath's promises to Alan to not get involved, Heath can't resist investigating a shopkeeper's murder in Chicago, which dashes their plans for a romantic weekend getaway. (978-1-163555-329-1)

Of Echoes Born by 'Nathan Burgoine. A collection of queer fantasy short stories set in Canada from Lambda Literary Award finalist 'Nathan Burgoine. (978-1-63555-096-2)

The Lurid Sea by Tom Cardamone. Cursed to spend eternity on his knees, Nerites is having the time of his life. (978-1-62639-911-2)

Sinister Justice by Steve Pickens. When a vigilante targets citizens of Jake Finnigan's hometown, Jake and his partner Sam fall under suspicion themselves as they investigate the murders. (978-1-63555-094-8)

Club Arcana: Operation Janus by Jon Wilson. Wizards, demons, Elder Gods: Who knew the universe was so crowded, and that they'd all be out to get Angus McAslan? (978-1-62639-969-3)

Triad Soul by 'Nathan Burgoine. Luc, Anders, and Curtis—vampire, demon, and wizard—must use their powers of blood, soul, and magic to defeat a murderer determined to turn their city into a battlefield. (978-1-62639-863-4)

Gatecrasher by Stephen Graham King. Aided by a high-tech thief, the Maverick Heart crew race against time to prevent a cadre of savage corporate mercenaries from seizing control of a revolutionary wormhole technology. (978-1-62639-936-5)

Wicked Frat Boy Ways by Todd Gregory. Beta Kappa brothers Brandon Benson and Phil Connor play an increasingly dangerous game of love, seduction, and emotional manipulation. (978-1-62639-671-5)

Death Goes Overboard by David S. Pederson. Heath Barrington and Alan Keyes are two sides of a steamy love triangle as they encounter gangsters, con men, murder, and more aboard an old lake steamer. (978-1-62639-907-5)

A Careful Heart by Ralph Josiah Bardsley. Be careful what you wish for…love changes everything. (978-1-62639-887-0)

Worms of Sin by Lyle Blake Smythers. A haunted mental asylum turned drug treatment facility exposes supernatural detective Finn M'Coul to an outbreak of murderous insanity, a strange parasite, and ghosts that seek sex with the living. (978-1-62639-823-8)

Tartarus by Eric Andrews-Katz. When Echidna, Mother of all Monsters, escapes from Tartarus and into the modern world, only an Olympian has the power to oppose her. (978-1-62639-746-0)

Rank by Richard Compson Sater. Rank means nothing to the heart, but the Air Force isn't as impartial. Every airman learns that rank has its privileges. What about love? (978-1-62639-845-0)

The Grim Reaper's Calling Card by Donald Webb. When Katsuro Tanaka begins investigating the disappearance of a young nurse, he discovers more missing persons, and they all have one thing in common: The Grim Reaper Tarot Card. (978-1-62639-748-4)

Smoldering Desires by C.E. Knipes. Evan McGarrity has found the man of his dreams in Sebastian Tantalos. When an old boyfriend from Sebastian's past enters the picture, Evan must fight for the man he loves. (978-1-62639-714-9)

CPSIA information can be obtained
at www.ICGtesting.com
Printed in the USA
LVHW040029210820
663761LV00004B/345